MEET THE SUPER DUPER SEVEN

TiM HAMILTON

HOLIDAY HOUSE · NEW YORK

DEDICATED TO EVERYONE WHO IS WILLING TO GIVE PEOPLE A SECOND, THIRD, AND FOURTH CHANCE!

Printed and bound in February 2022 at C&C Offset, Shenzhen, China.
The artwork was created with pen and ink, watercolor, and digital tools.
www.holidayhouse.com

First Edition
1 3 5 7 9 10 8 6 4 2

Library of Congress Cataloging-in-Publication Data
Names: Hamilton, Tim, author, illustrator.
Title: Meet the Super Duper Seven / Tim Hamilton.
Description: First edition. | New York : Holiday House, [2022] | Series: I like to read comics | Audience: Ages 6-8 | Audience: Grades K-1 | Summary: The Super Duper Seven are holding auditions for their crime-fighting superhero club but Hungry Kitty keeps eating members of the team.
Identifiers: LCCN 2021034062 | ISBN 9780823449101 (hardcover)
Subjects: CYAC: Graphic novels. | Humorous stories. | Animals—Fiction
Ability—Fiction. | Clubs—Fiction. | LCGFT: Graphic novels. | Funny animal comics.
Classification: LCC PZ7.7 .H3617 2022 | DDC 741.5/973—dc23
LC record available at https://lccn.loc.gov/2021034062

ISBN: 978-0-8234-4910-1 (Hardcover)

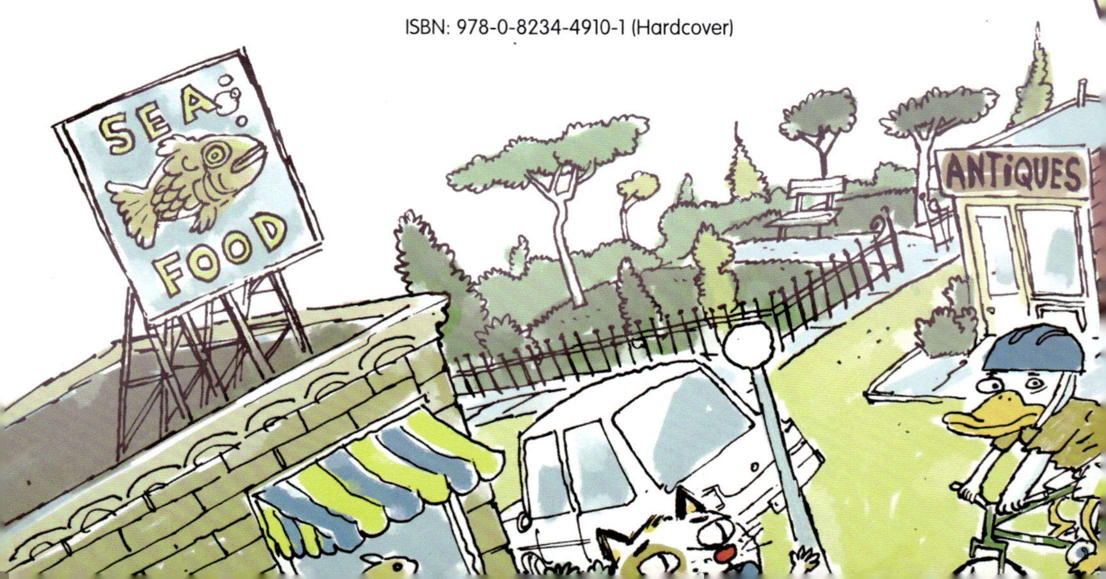
SEA FOOD
ANTIQUES

ONE DAY . . .

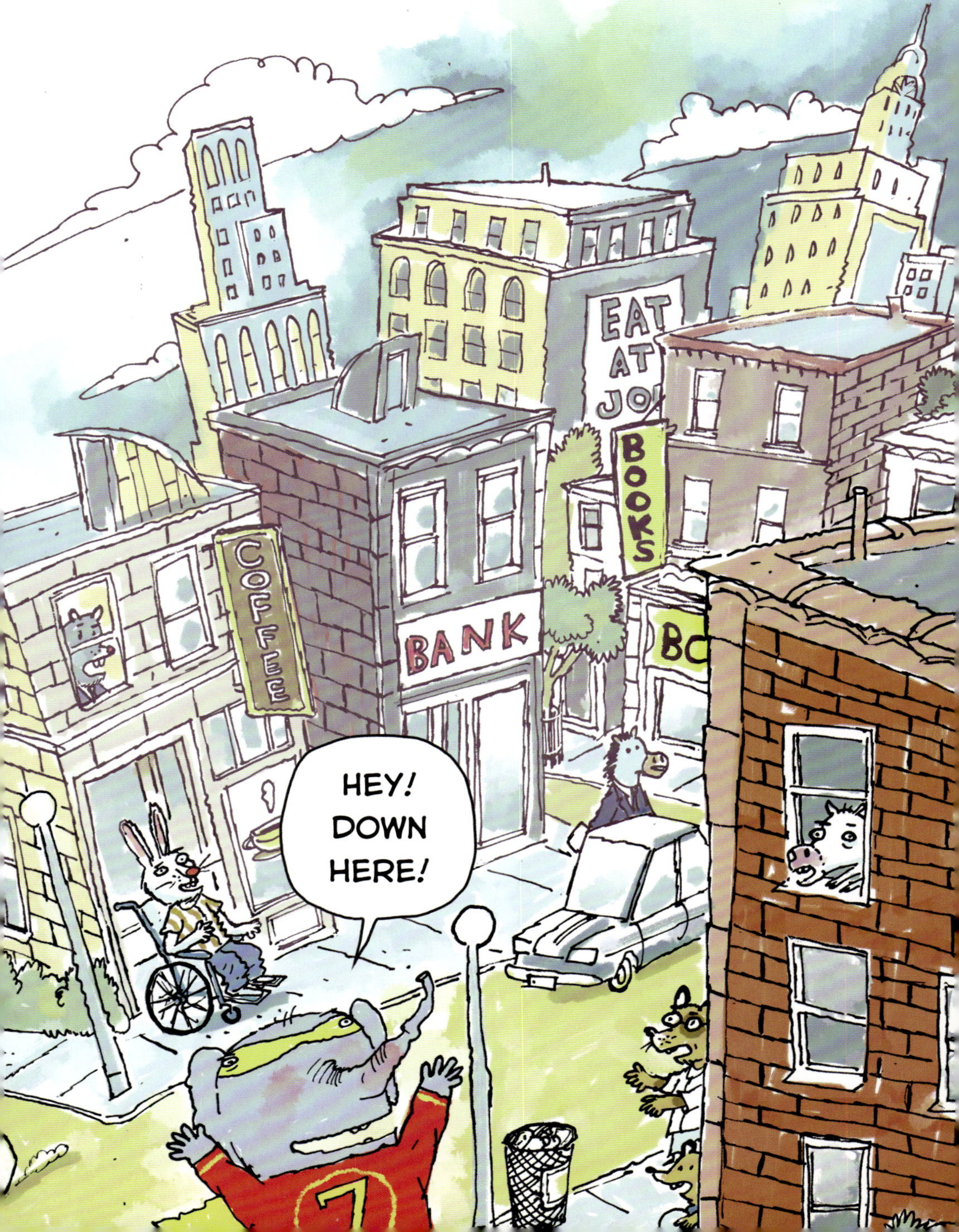
EAT AT JO
BOOKS
COFFEE
BANK
BO
HEY! DOWN HERE!

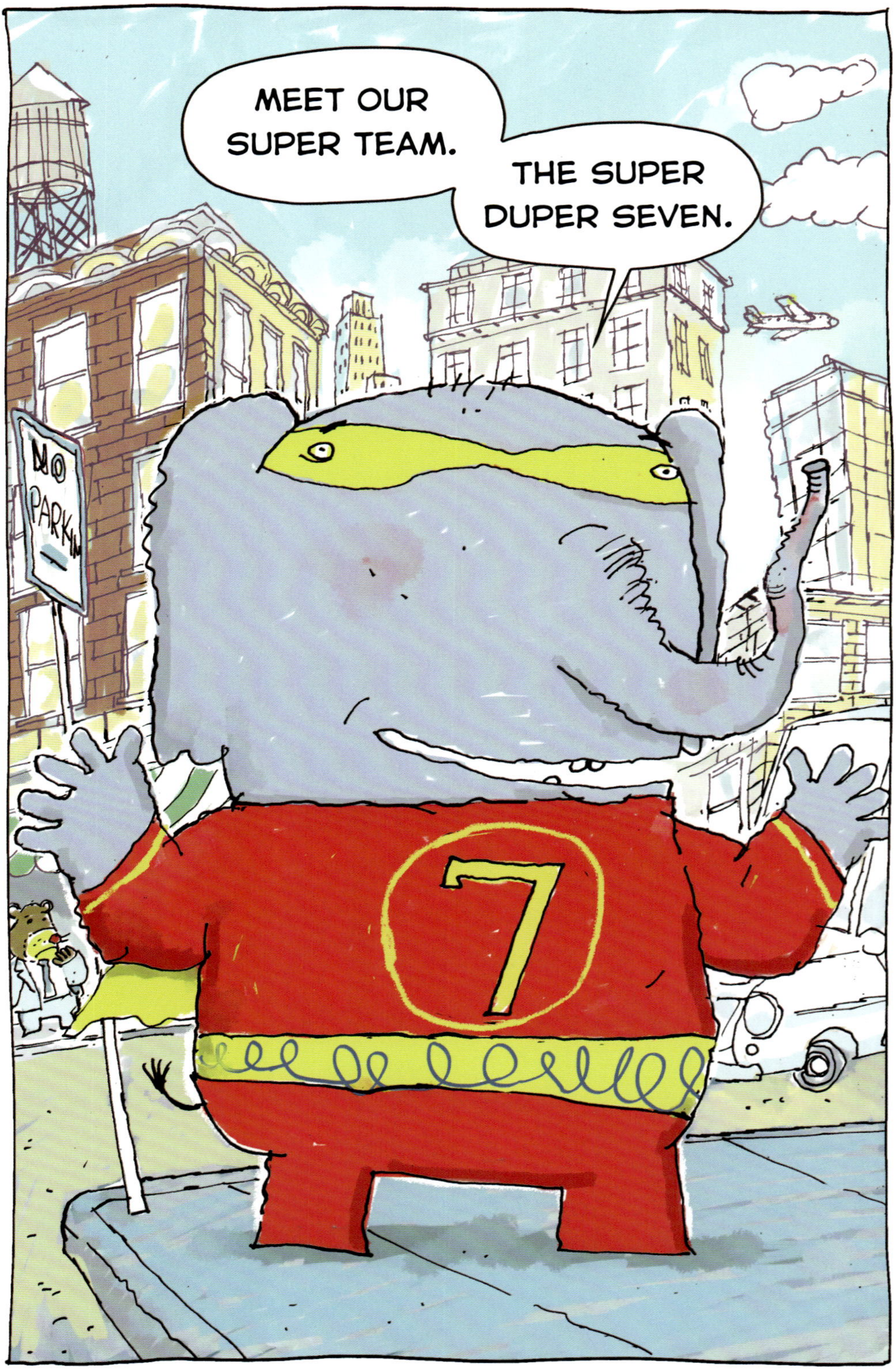
MEET OUR SUPER TEAM.
THE SUPER DUPER SEVEN.
NO PARKIN
7

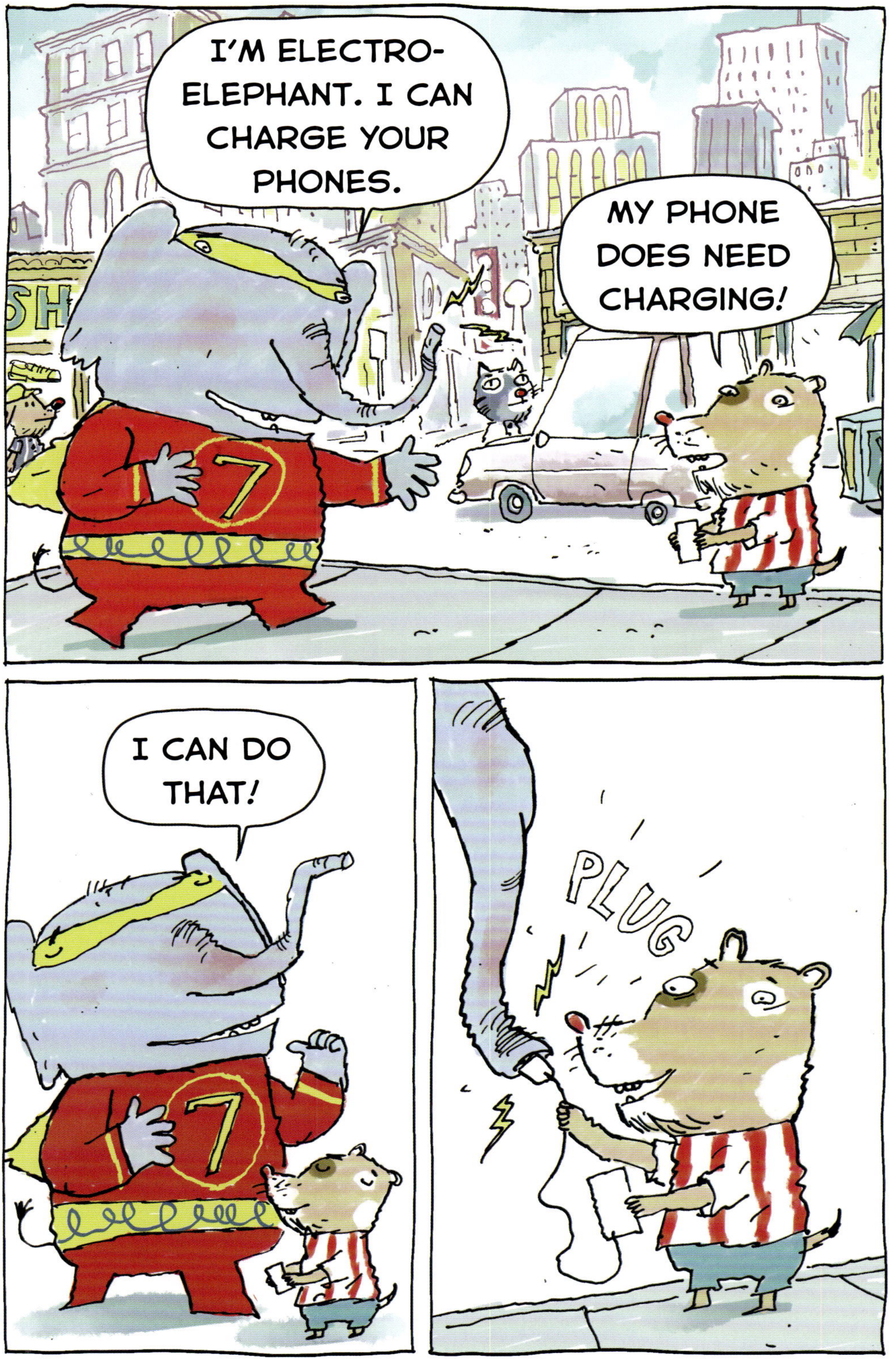
I'M ELECTRO-ELEPHANT. I CAN CHARGE YOUR PHONES.
MY PHONE DOES NEED CHARGING!
I CAN DO THAT!
PLUG

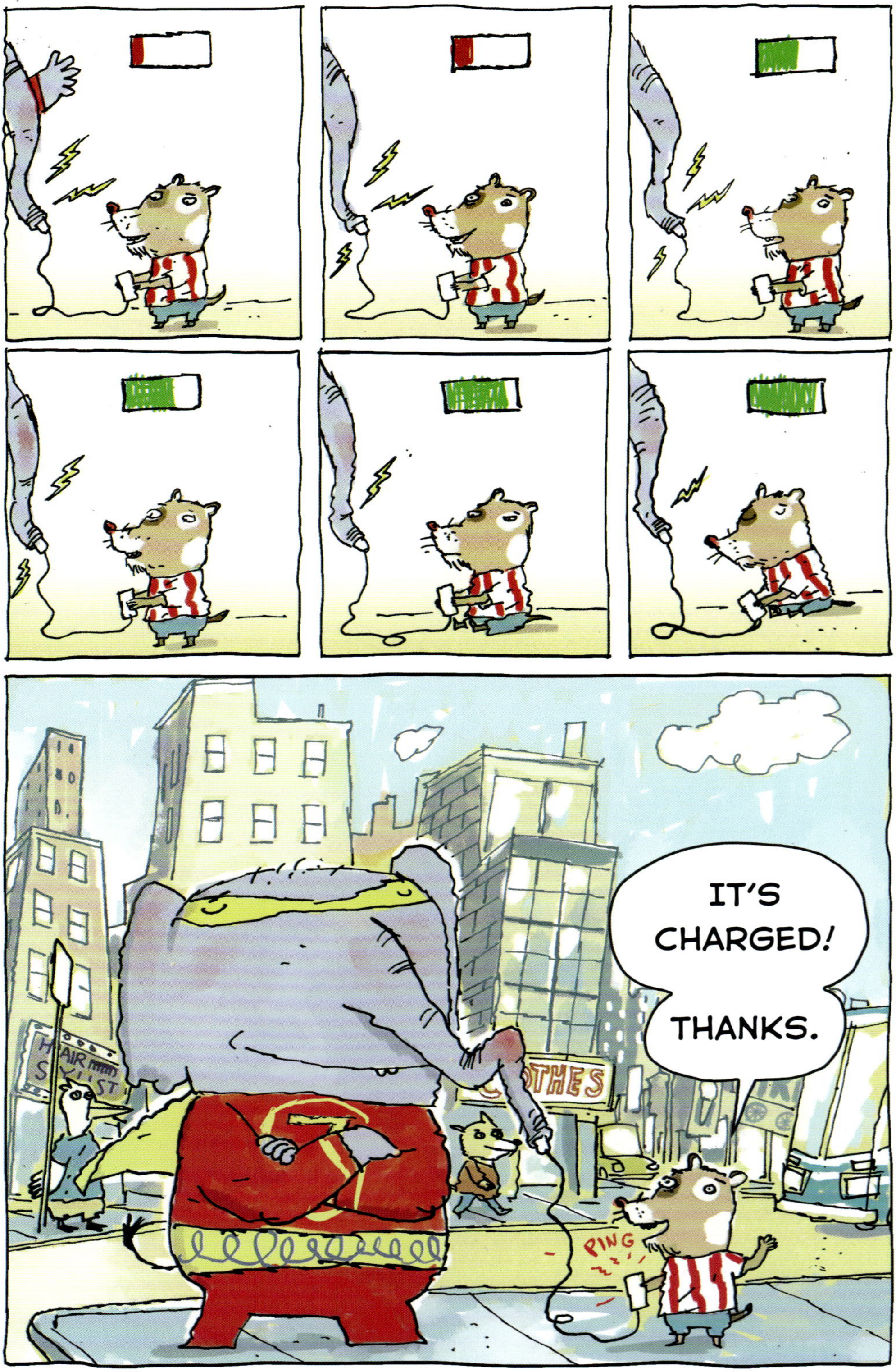
IT'S CHARGED!
THANKS.
PING

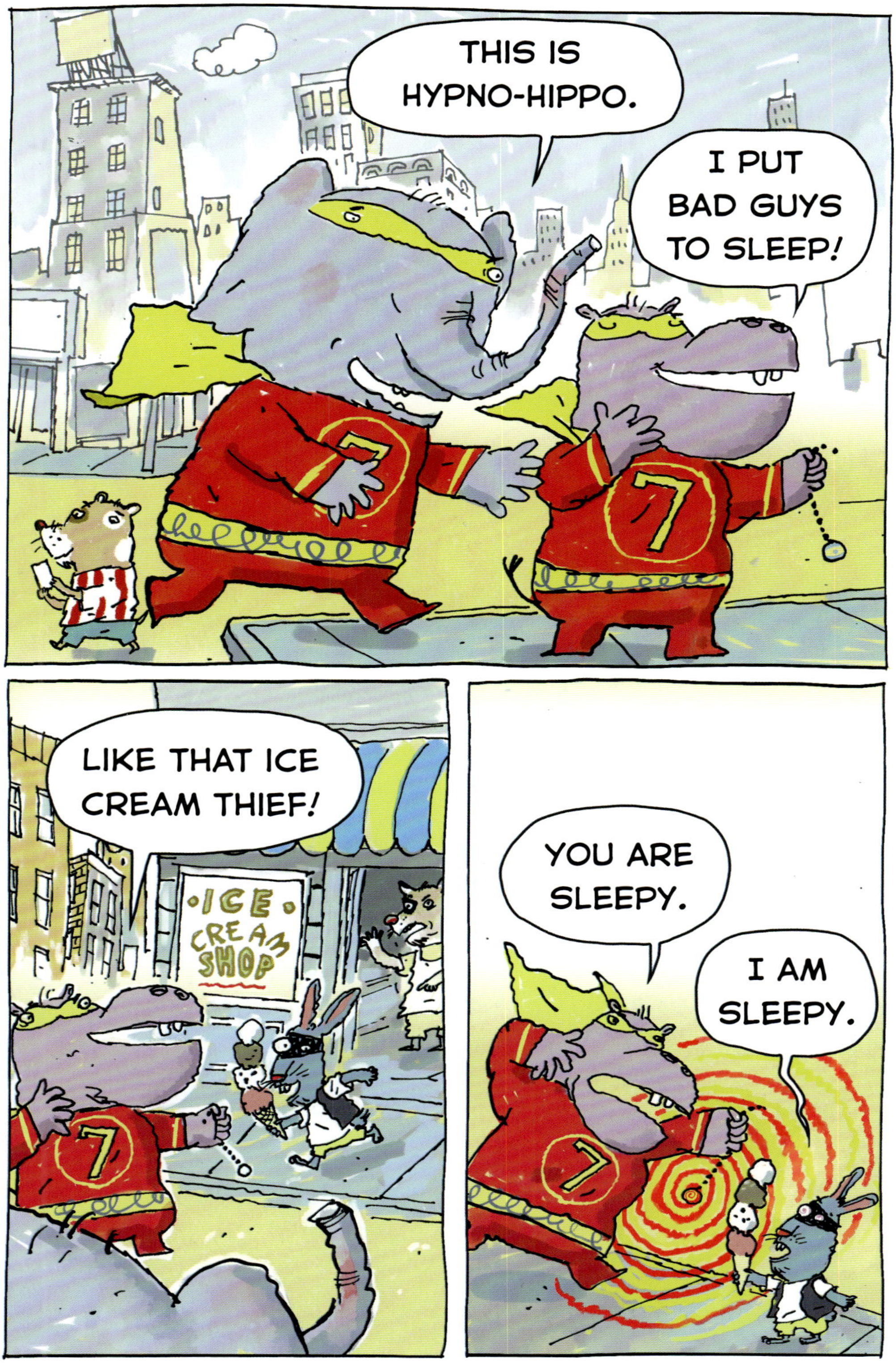
THIS IS HYPNO-HIPPO.
I PUT BAD GUYS TO SLEEP!
LIKE THAT ICE CREAM THIEF!
ICE CREAM SHOP
YOU ARE SLEEPY.
I AM SLEEPY.

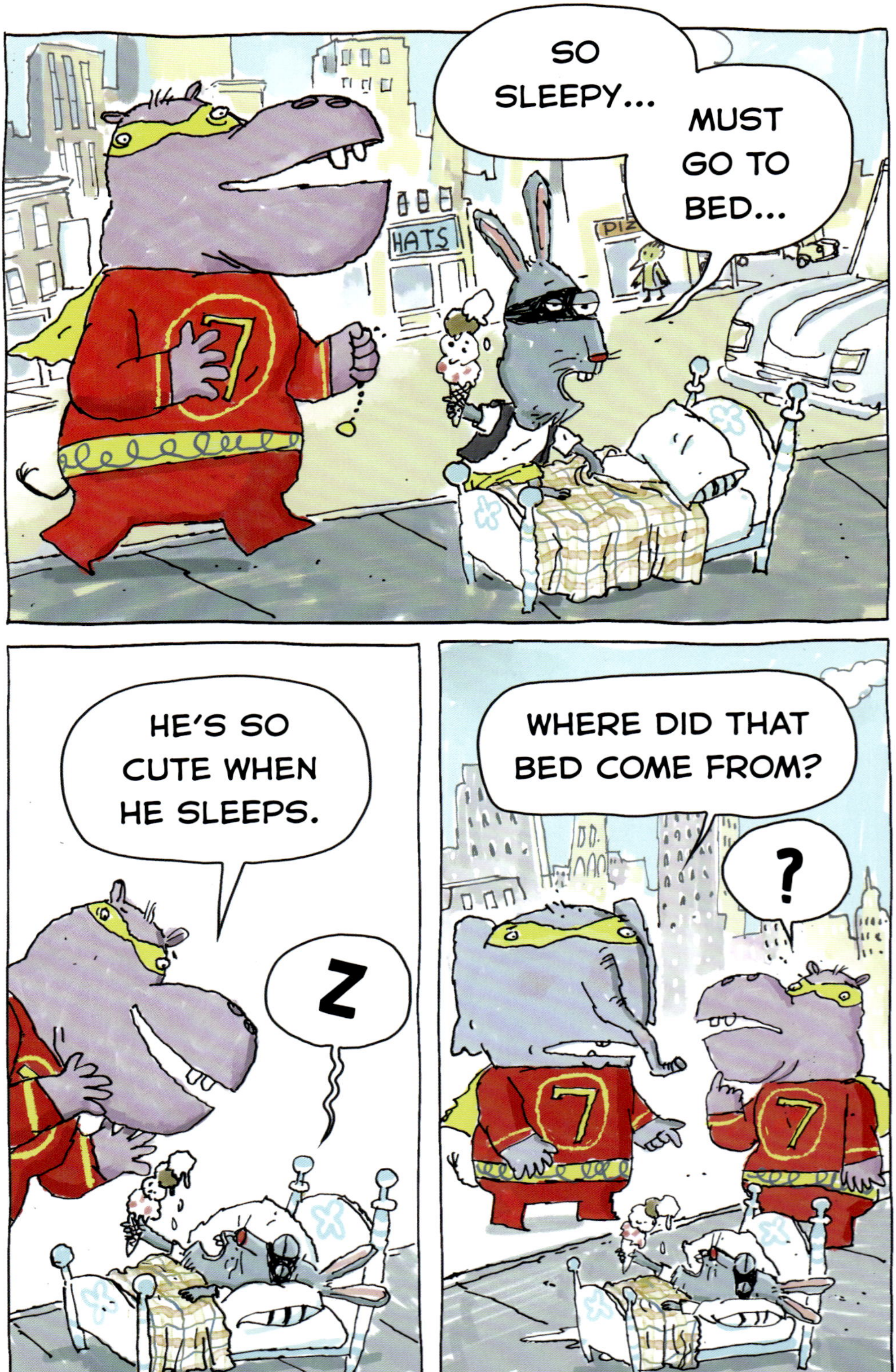
SO SLEEPY...
MUST GO TO BED...
HATS
HE'S SO CUTE WHEN HE SLEEPS.
Z
WHERE DID THAT BED COME FROM?
?

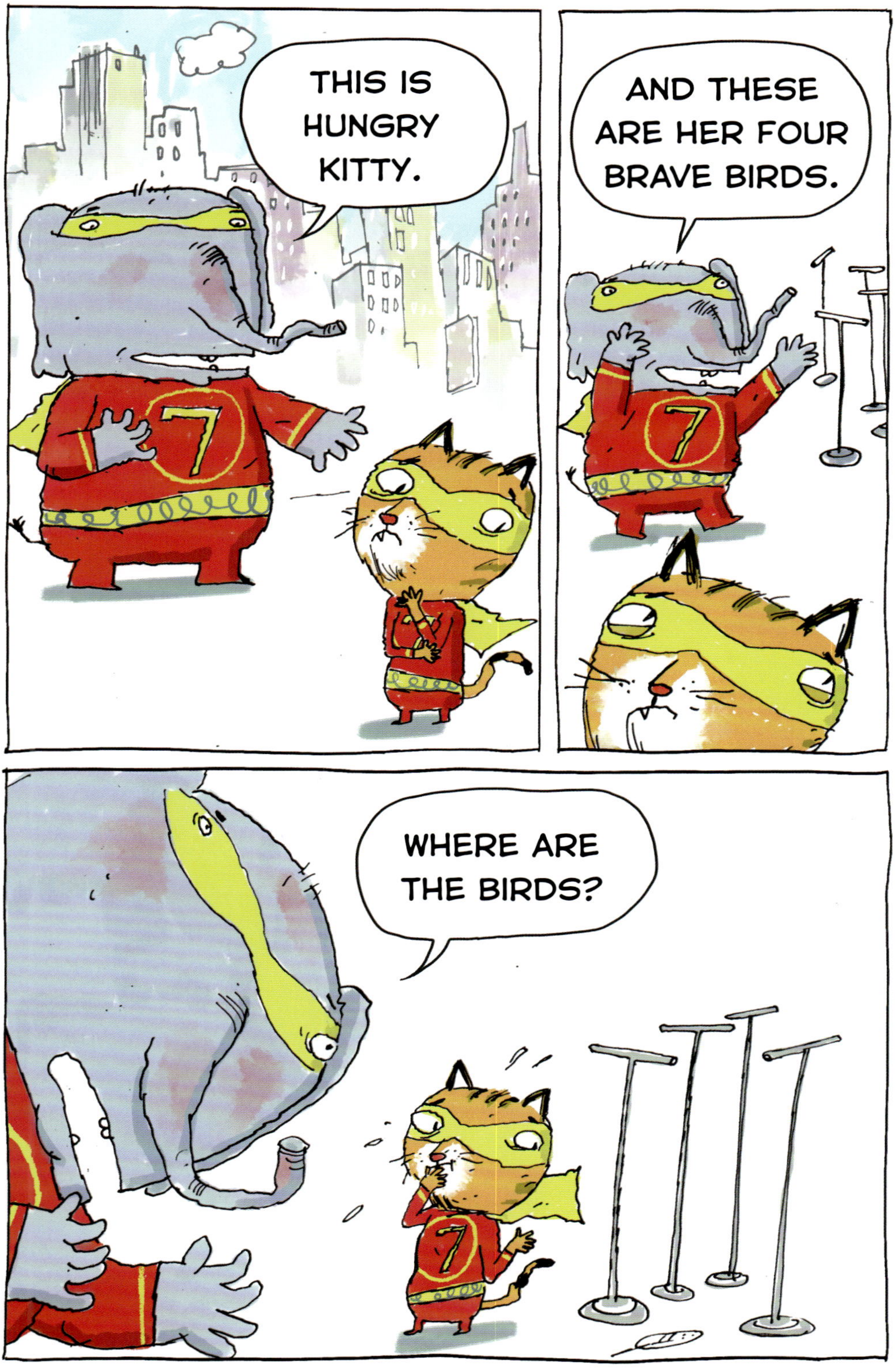
THIS IS HUNGRY KITTY.
AND THESE ARE HER FOUR BRAVE BIRDS.
WHERE ARE THE BIRDS?

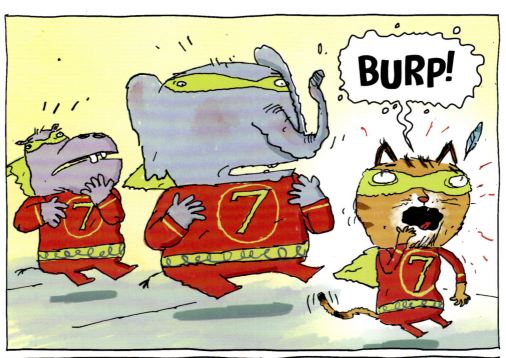

BURP!

YOU ATE THEM? BUT THEY'RE ON THE COVER OF OUR BOOK!

I'M HUNGRY! MY NAME *IS* HUNGRY KITTY!

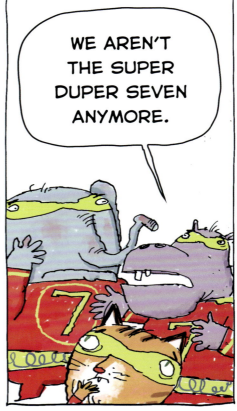

WE AREN'T THE SUPER DUPER SEVEN ANYMORE.

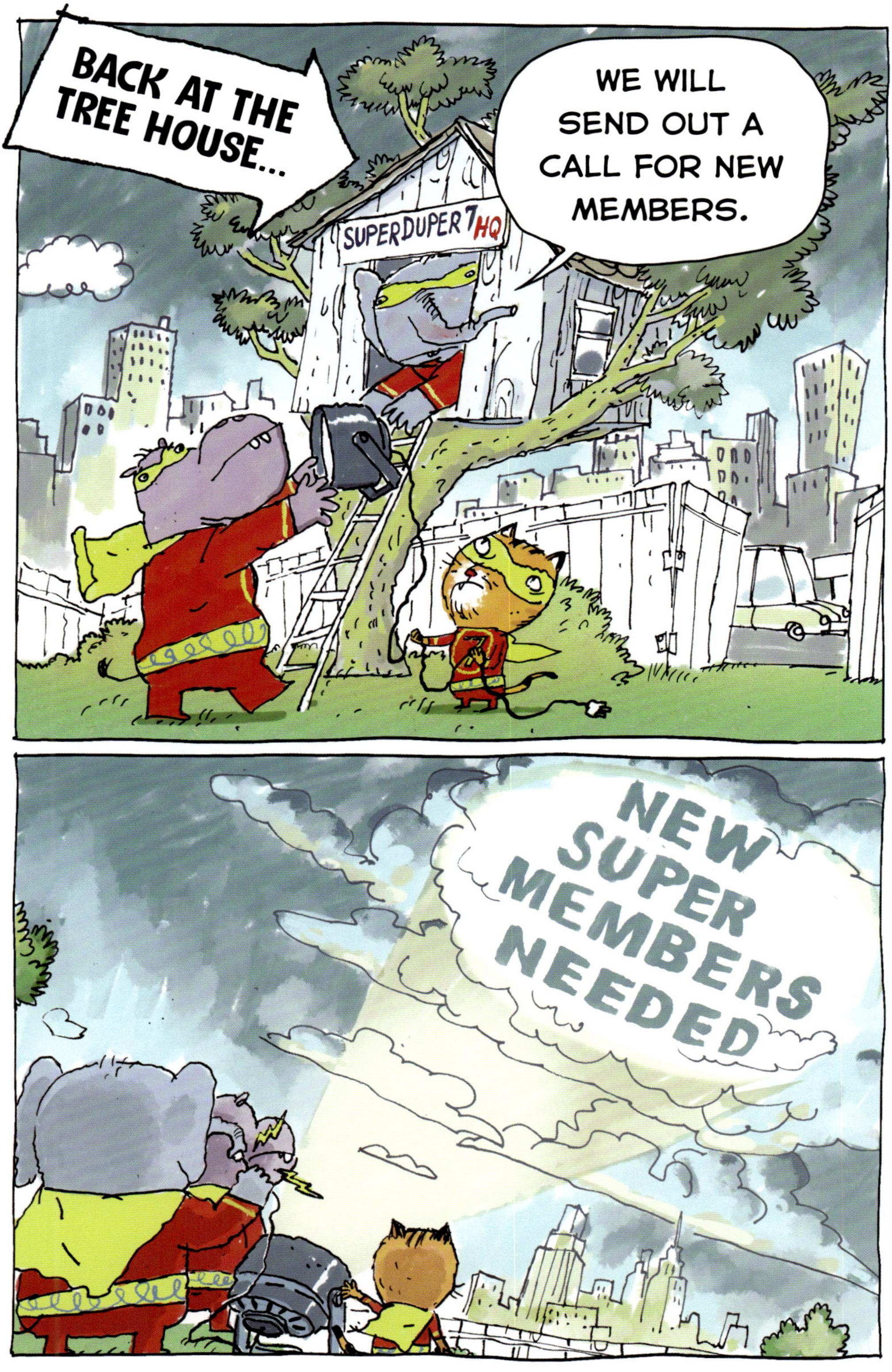
BACK AT THE TREE HOUSE...
WE WILL SEND OUT A CALL FOR NEW MEMBERS.
SUPERDUPER 7 HQ
NEW SUPER MEMBERS NEEDED

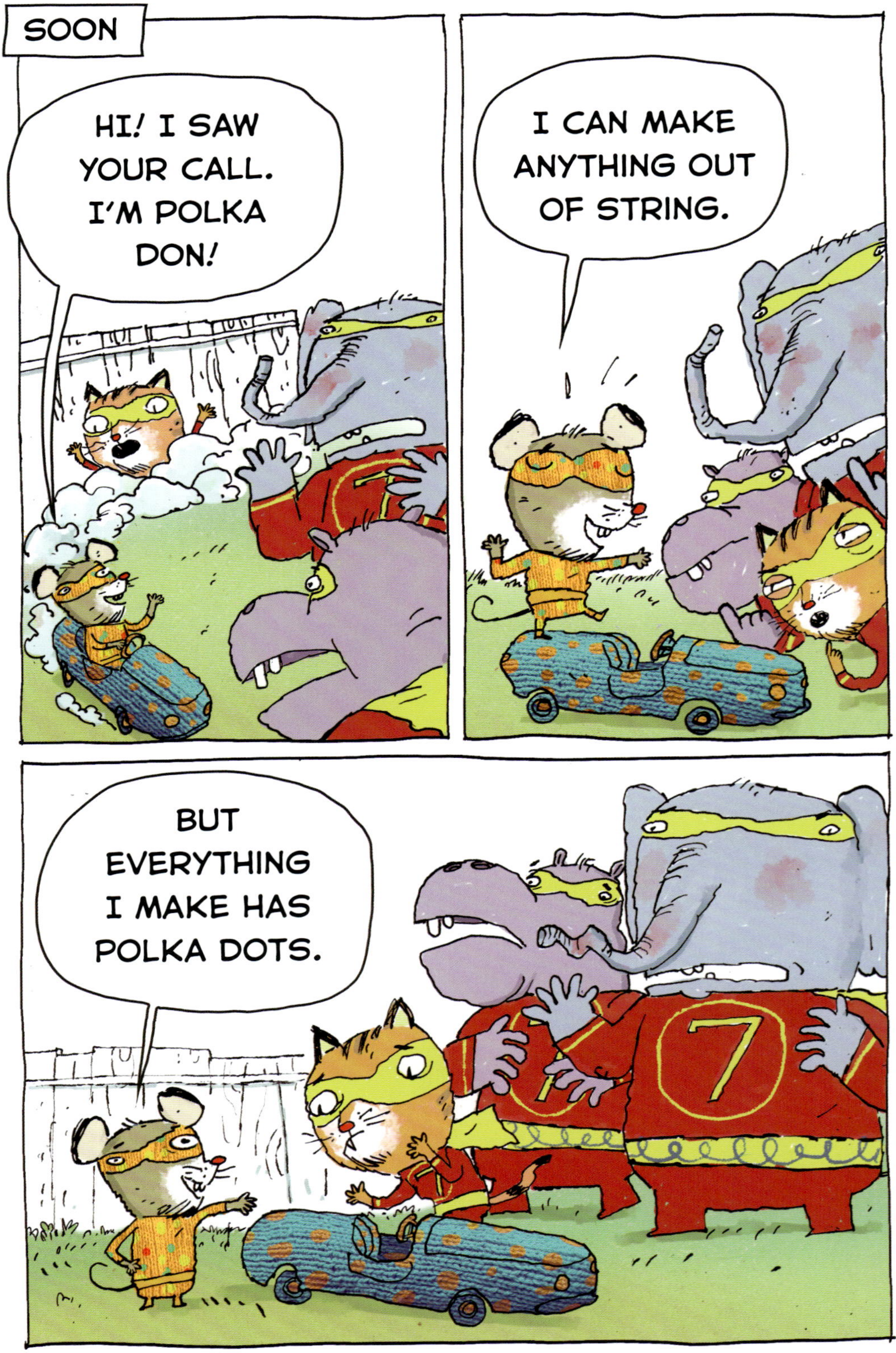
SOON
HI! I SAW YOUR CALL. I'M POLKA DON!
I CAN MAKE ANYTHING OUT OF STRING.
BUT EVERYTHING I MAKE HAS POLKA DOTS.

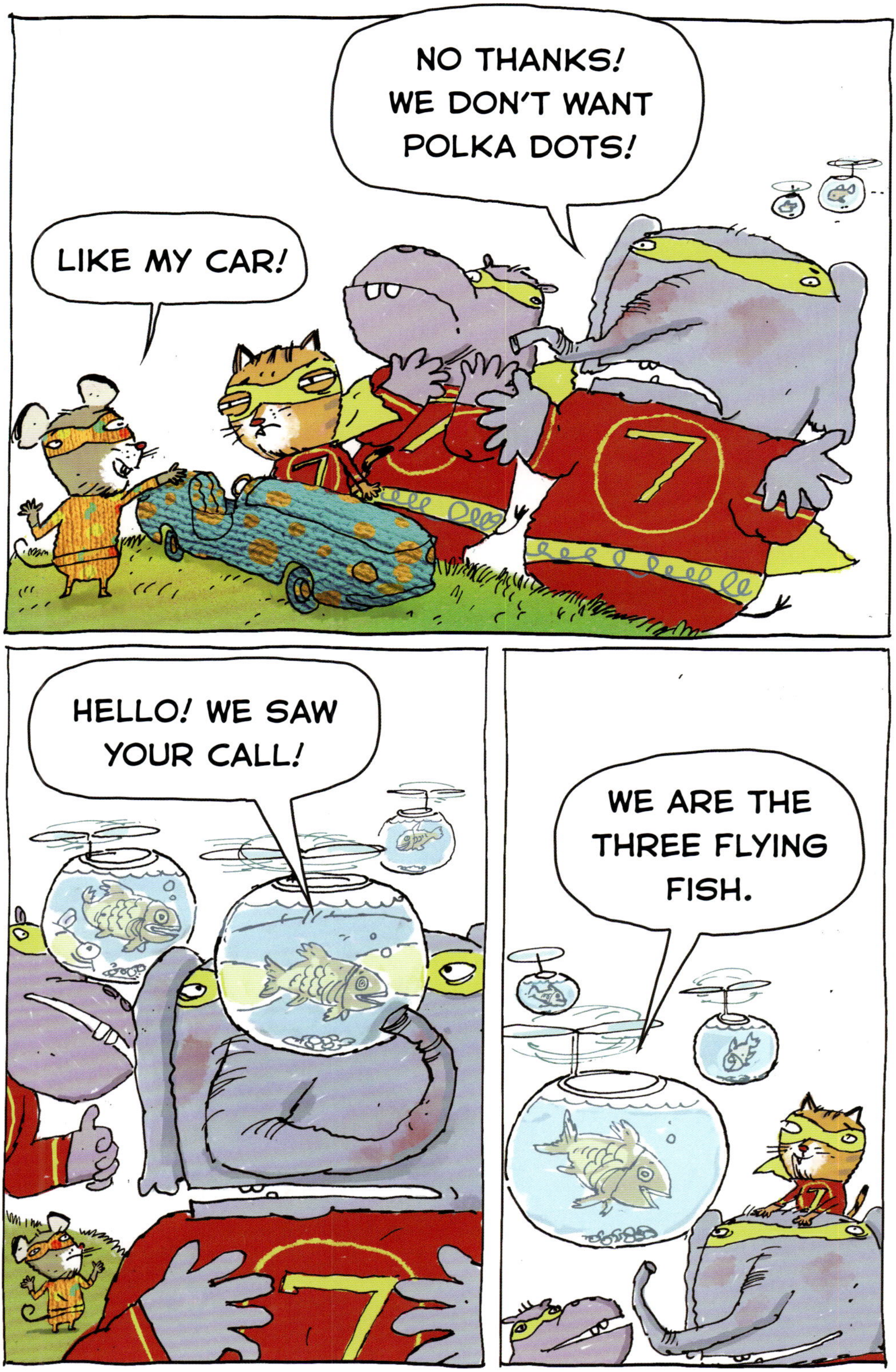
LIKE MY CAR!
NO THANKS! WE DON'T WANT POLKA DOTS!
HELLO! WE SAW YOUR CALL!
WE ARE THE THREE FLYING FISH.

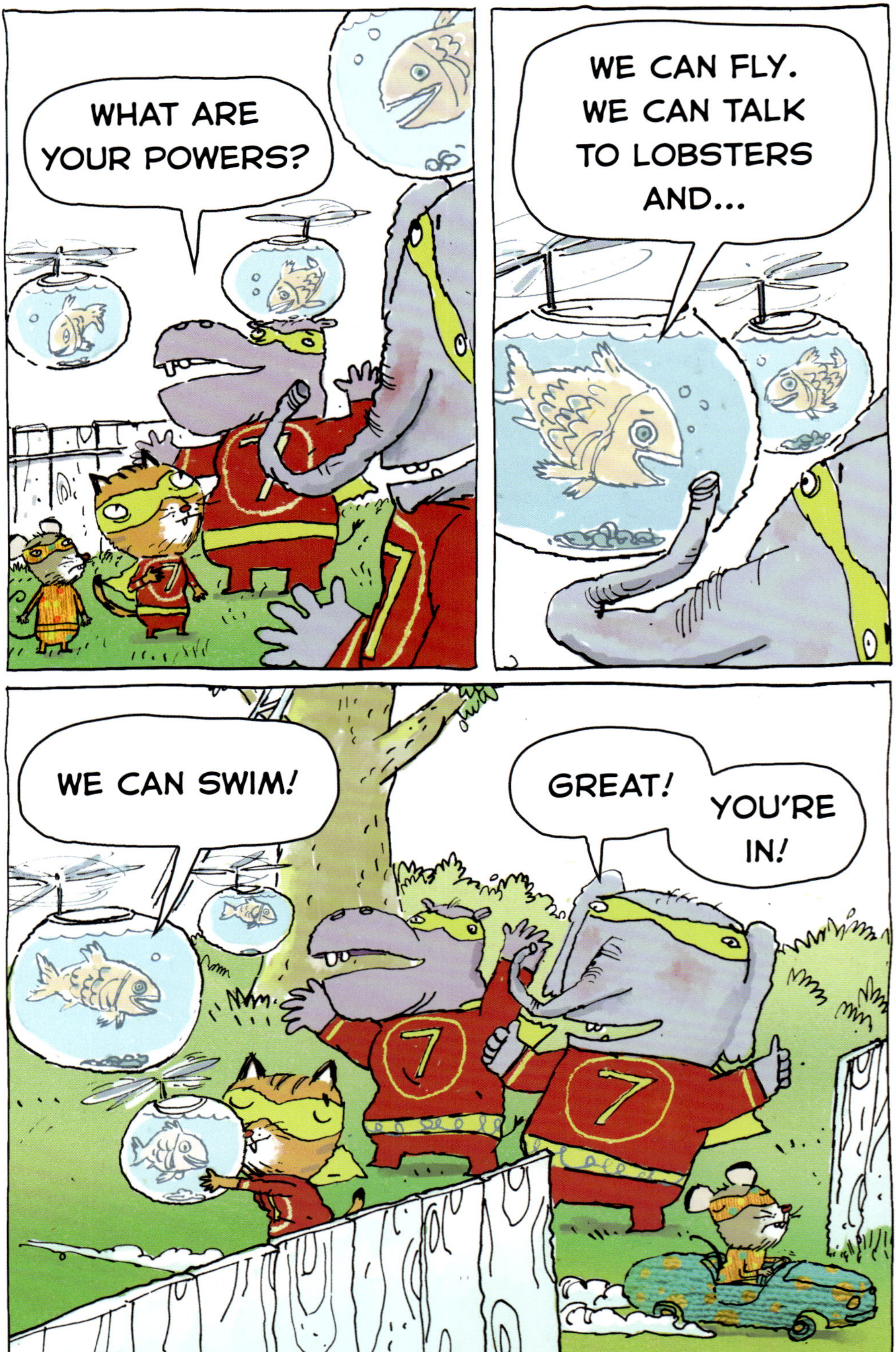
WHAT ARE YOUR POWERS?
WE CAN FLY. WE CAN TALK TO LOBSTERS AND...
WE CAN SWIM!
GREAT!
YOU'RE IN!

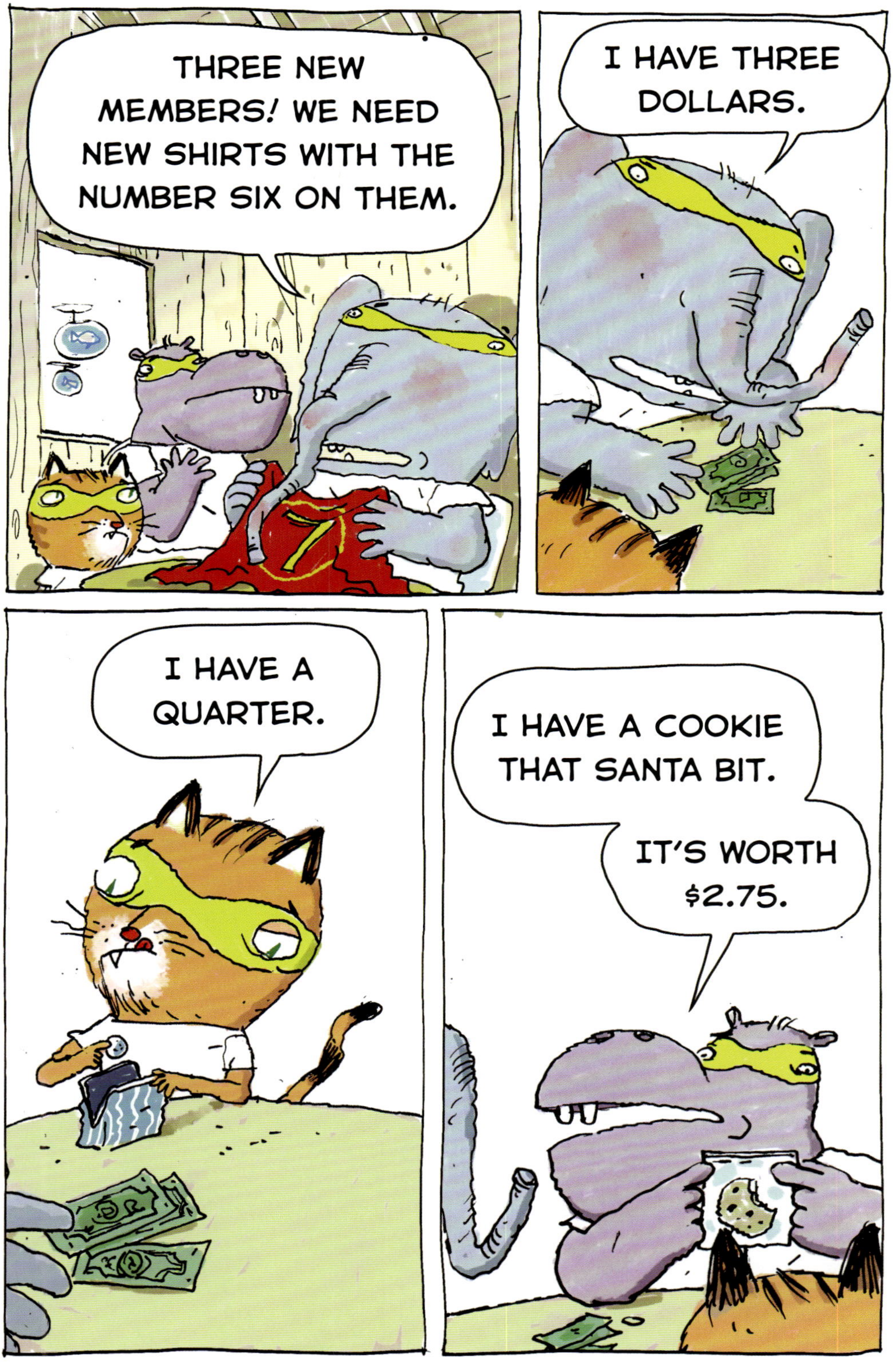
THREE NEW MEMBERS! WE NEED NEW SHIRTS WITH THE NUMBER SIX ON THEM.
I HAVE THREE DOLLARS.
I HAVE A QUARTER.
I HAVE A COOKIE THAT SANTA BIT.
IT'S WORTH $2.75.

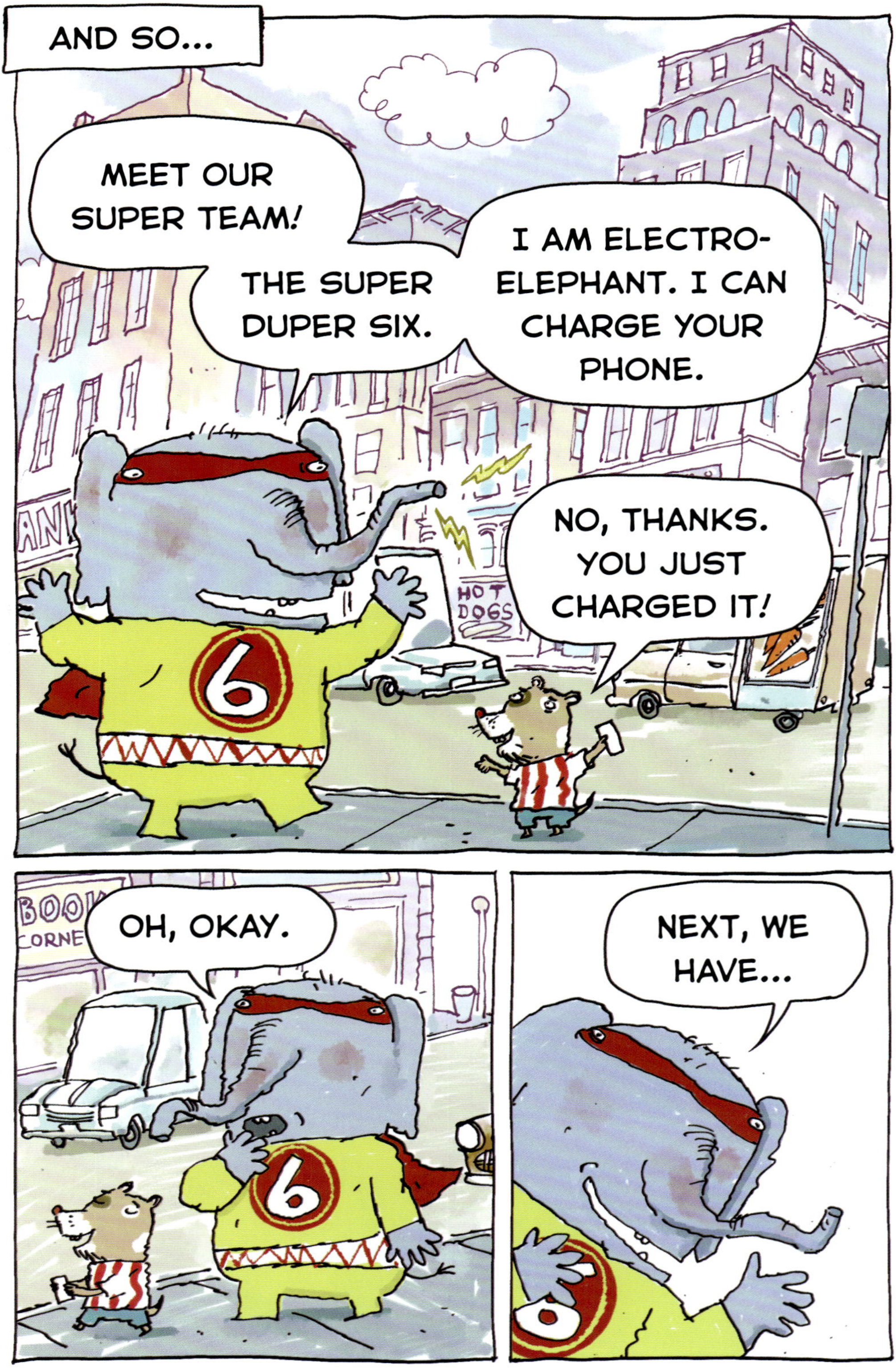
AND SO...
MEET OUR SUPER TEAM!
THE SUPER DUPER SIX.
I AM ELECTRO-ELEPHANT. I CAN CHARGE YOUR PHONE.
NO, THANKS. YOU JUST CHARGED IT!
HOT DOGS
BOOK CORNE
OH, OKAY.
NEXT, WE HAVE...

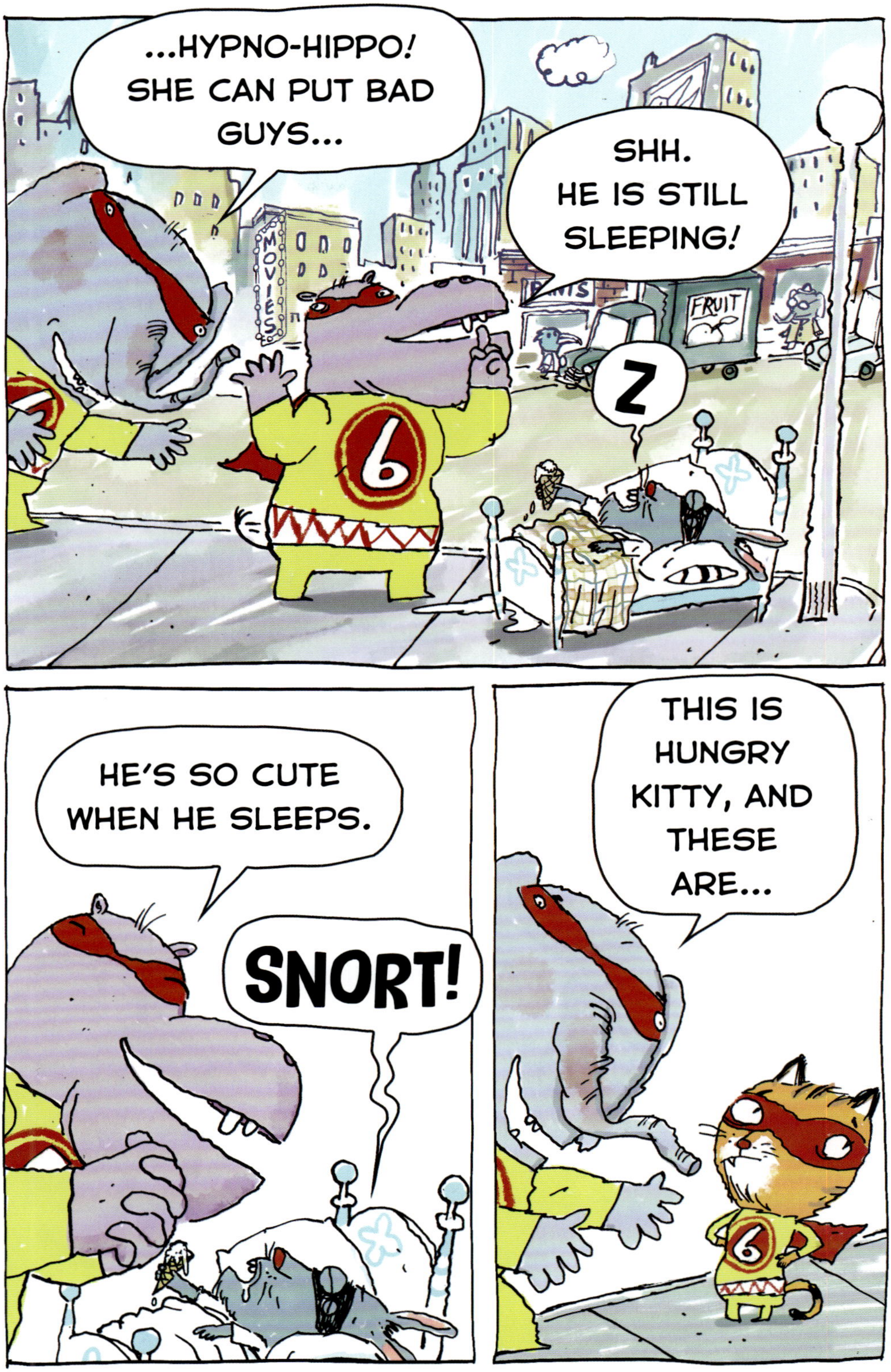
...HYPNO-HIPPO! SHE CAN PUT BAD GUYS...
SHH. HE IS STILL SLEEPING!
MOVIES
FRUIT
Z
HE'S SO CUTE WHEN HE SLEEPS.
SNORT!
THIS IS HUNGRY KITTY, AND THESE ARE...

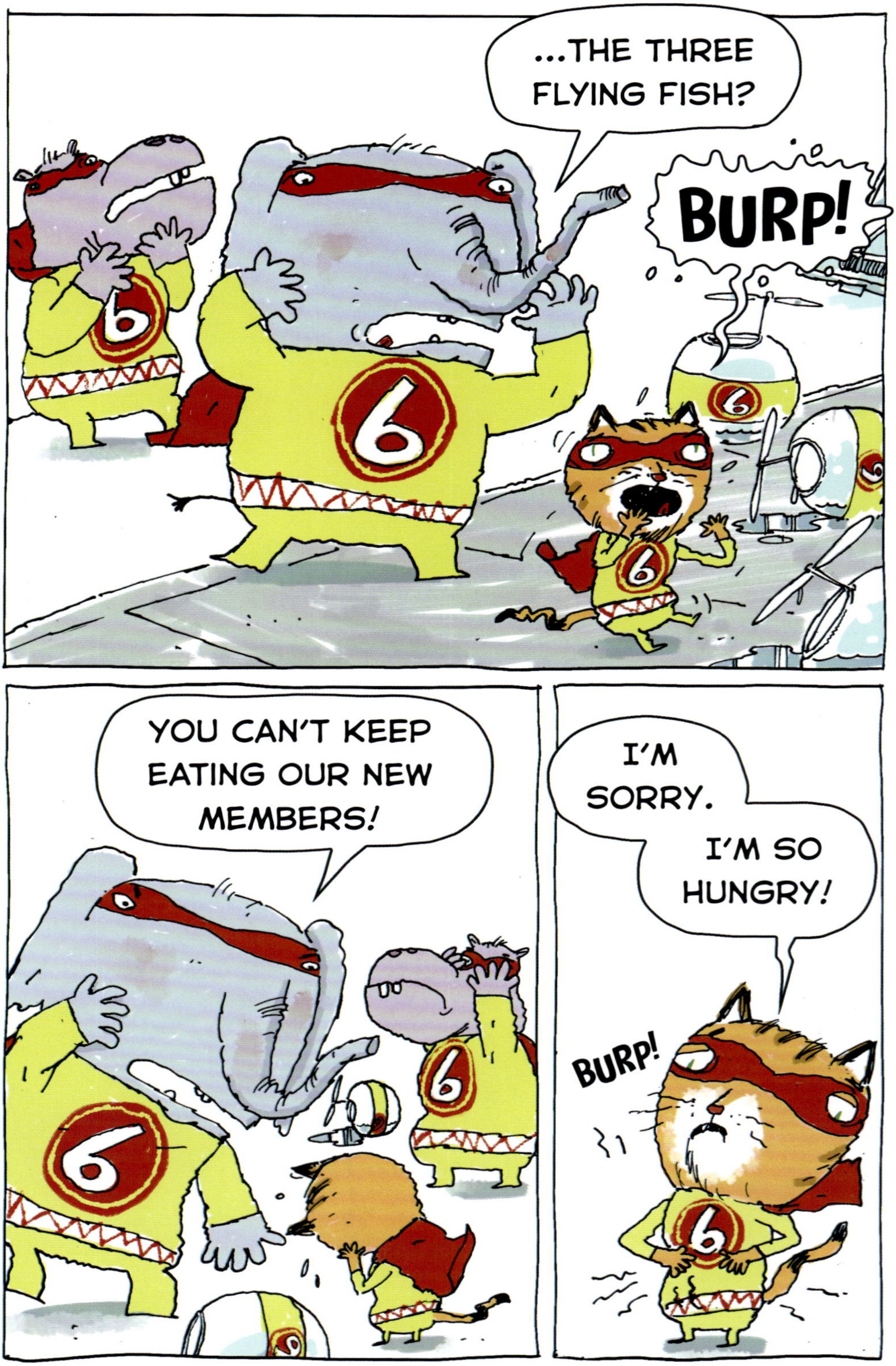
...THE THREE FLYING FISH?
BURP!
YOU CAN'T KEEP EATING OUR NEW MEMBERS!
I'M SORRY.
I'M SO HUNGRY!
BURP!

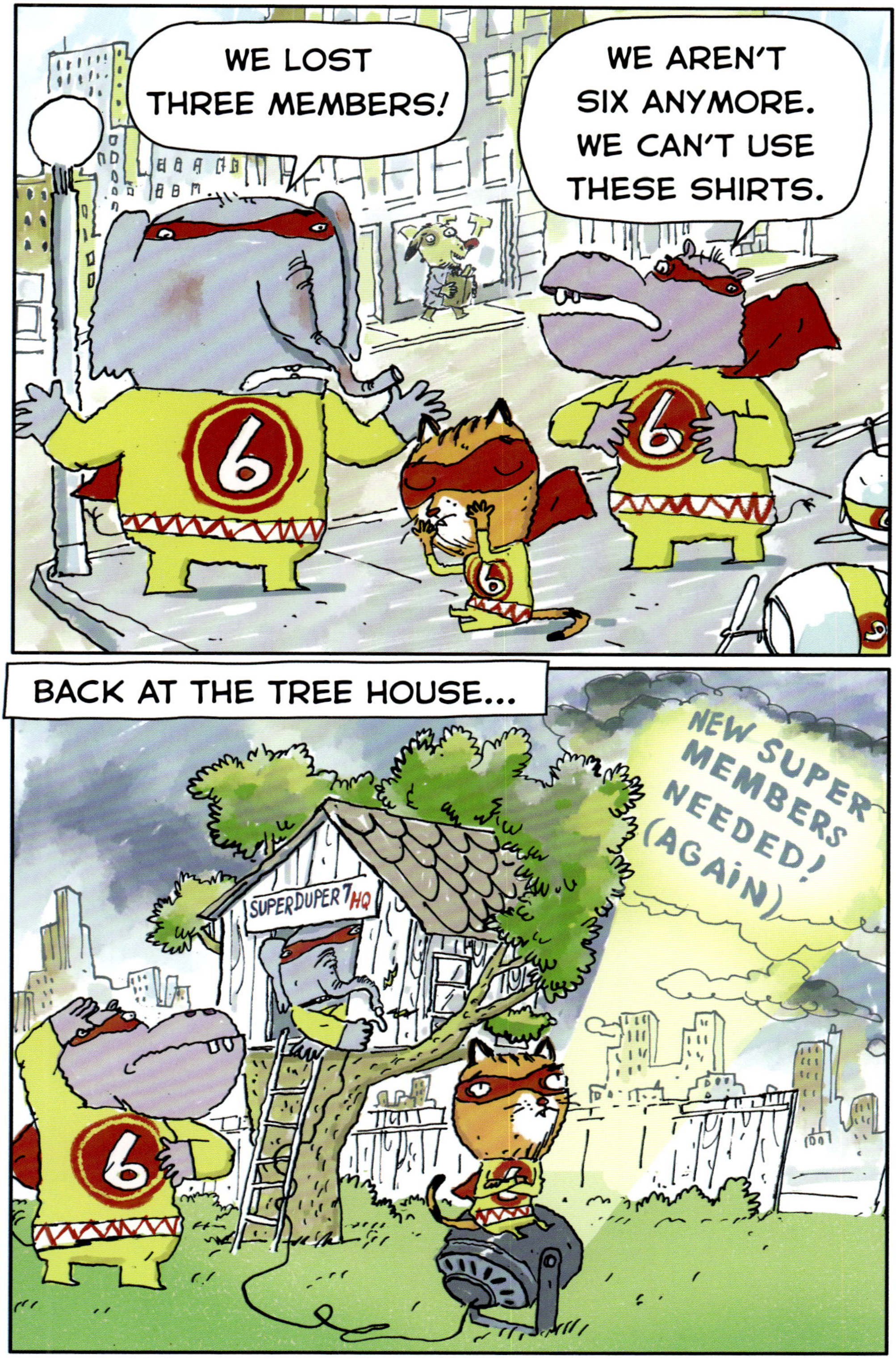
WE LOST THREE MEMBERS!
WE AREN'T SIX ANYMORE. WE CAN'T USE THESE SHIRTS.
BACK AT THE TREE HOUSE...
SUPERDUPER 7 HQ
NEW SUPER MEMBERS NEEDED! (AGAIN)

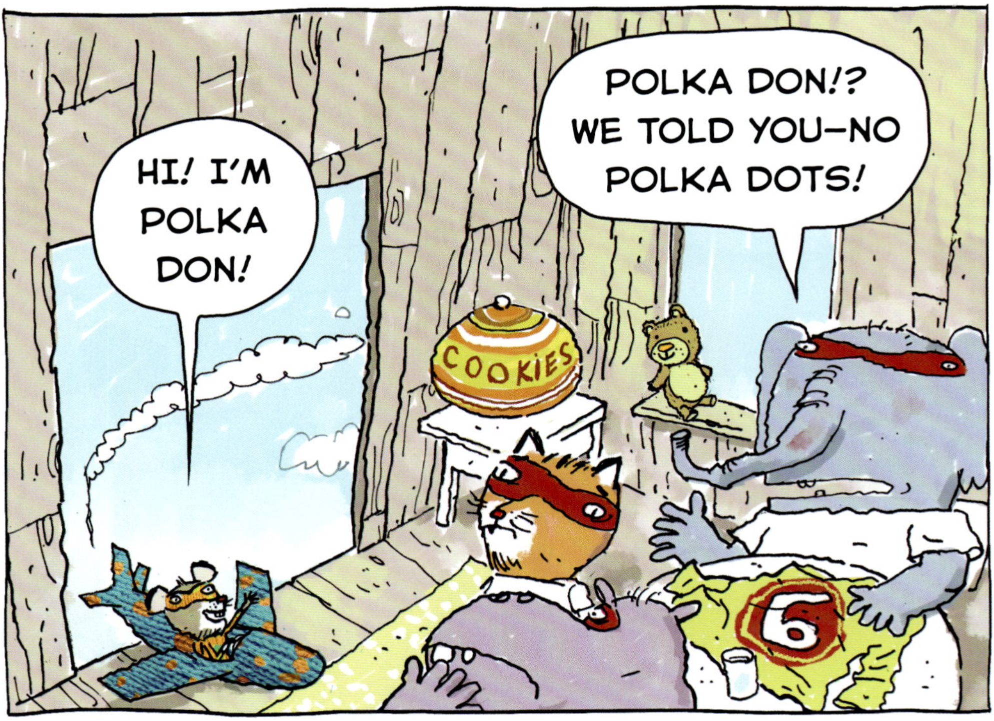
HI! I'M POLKA DON!
POLKA DON!? WE TOLD YOU—NO POLKA DOTS!
COOKIES
6

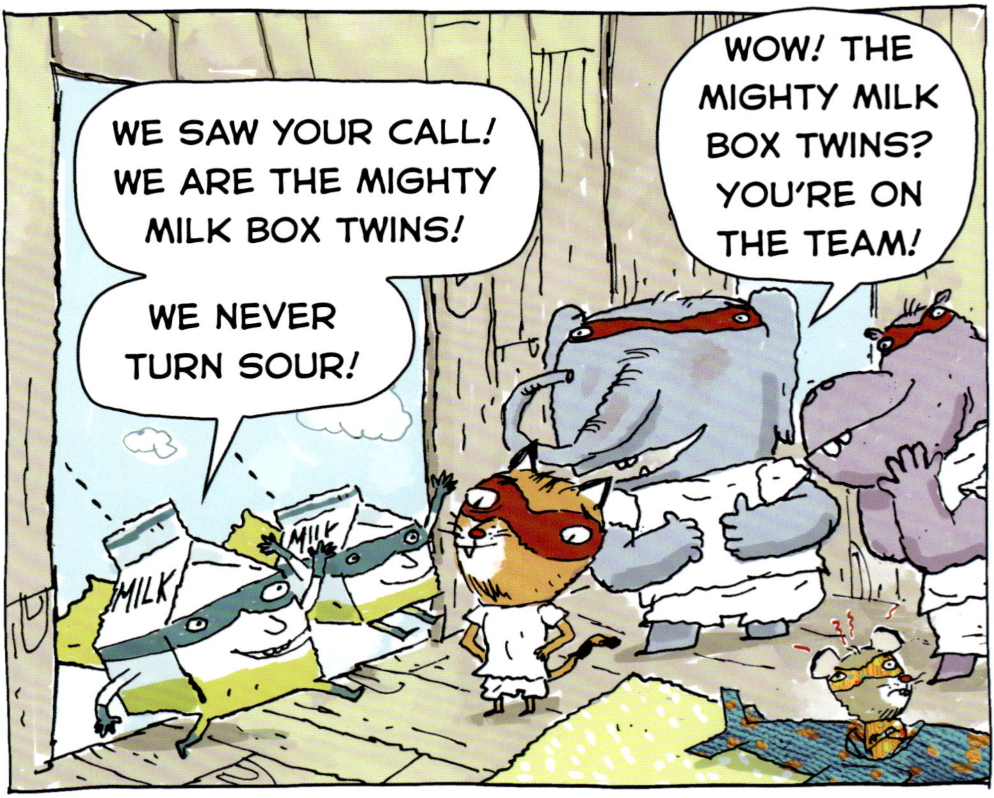
WE SAW YOUR CALL! WE ARE THE MIGHTY MILK BOX TWINS!
WE NEVER TURN SOUR!
WOW! THE MIGHTY MILK BOX TWINS? YOU'RE ON THE TEAM!
MILK
MILK

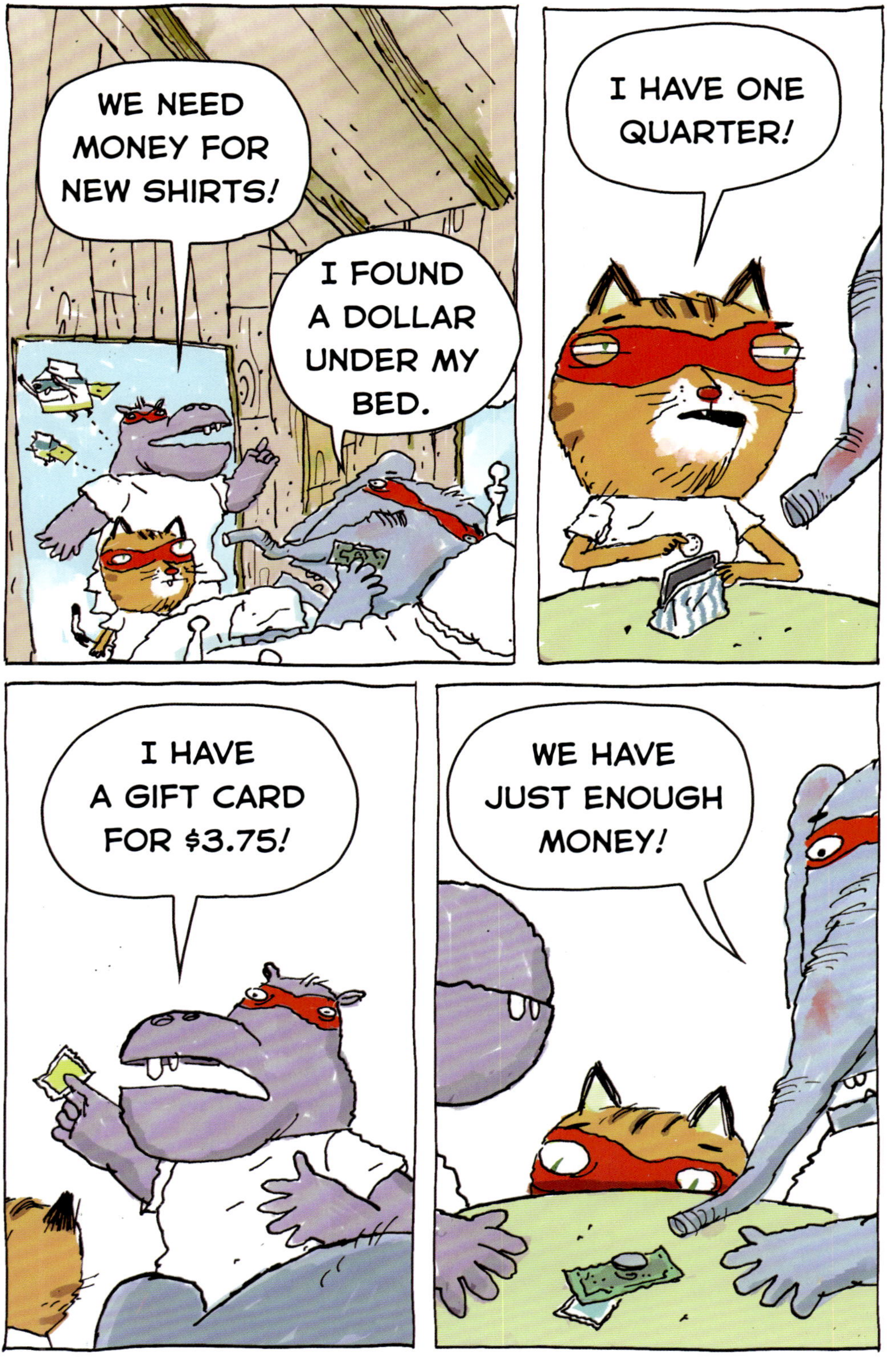
WE NEED MONEY FOR NEW SHIRTS!
I FOUND A DOLLAR UNDER MY BED.
I HAVE ONE QUARTER!
I HAVE A GIFT CARD FOR $3.75!
WE HAVE JUST ENOUGH MONEY!

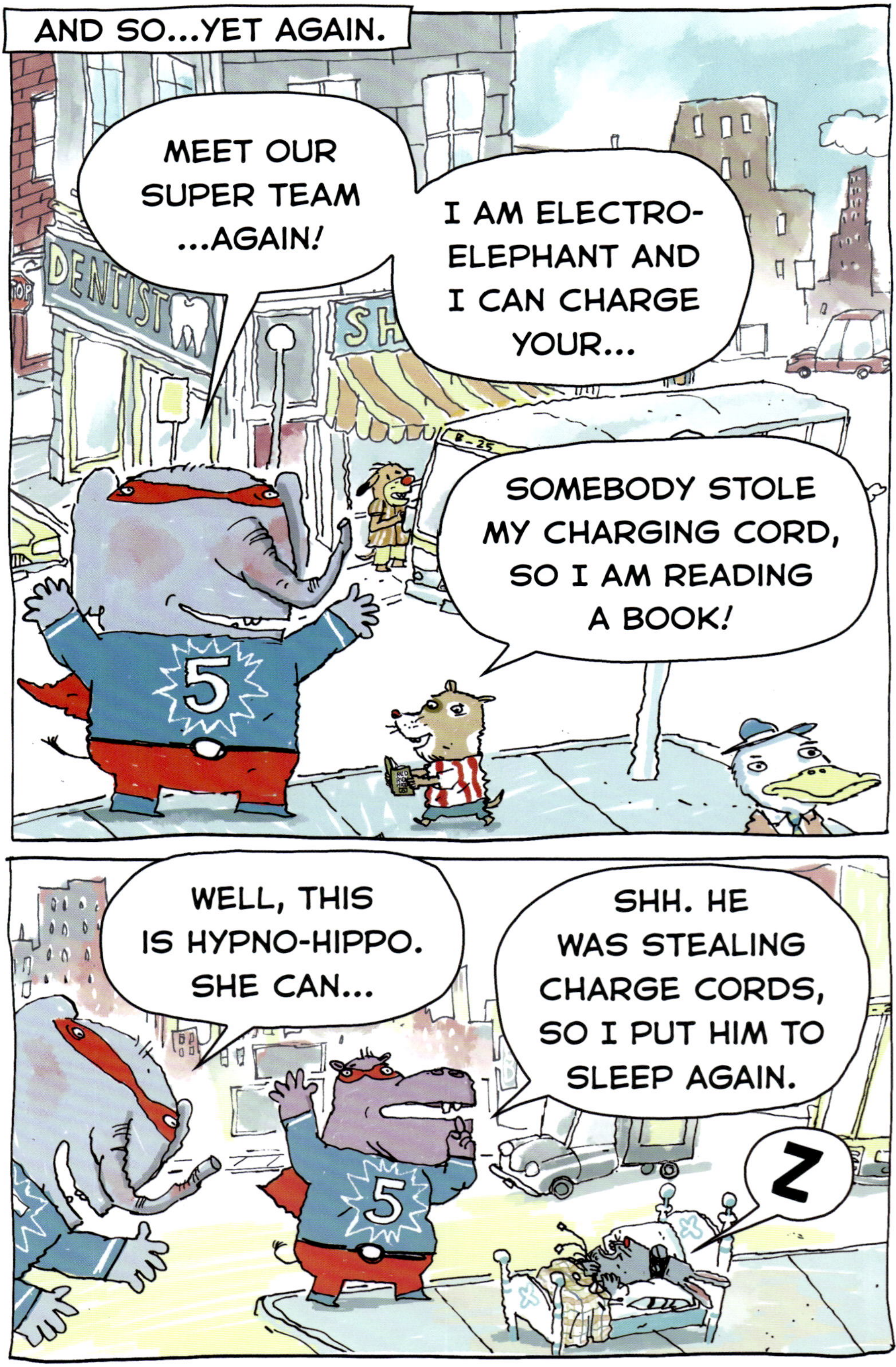
AND SO...YET AGAIN.
MEET OUR SUPER TEAM ...AGAIN!
I AM ELECTRO-ELEPHANT AND I CAN CHARGE YOUR...
DENTIST
SOMEBODY STOLE MY CHARGING CORD, SO I AM READING A BOOK!
5
WELL, THIS IS HYPNO-HIPPO. SHE CAN...
SHH. HE WAS STEALING CHARGE CORDS, SO I PUT HIM TO SLEEP AGAIN.
5
Z

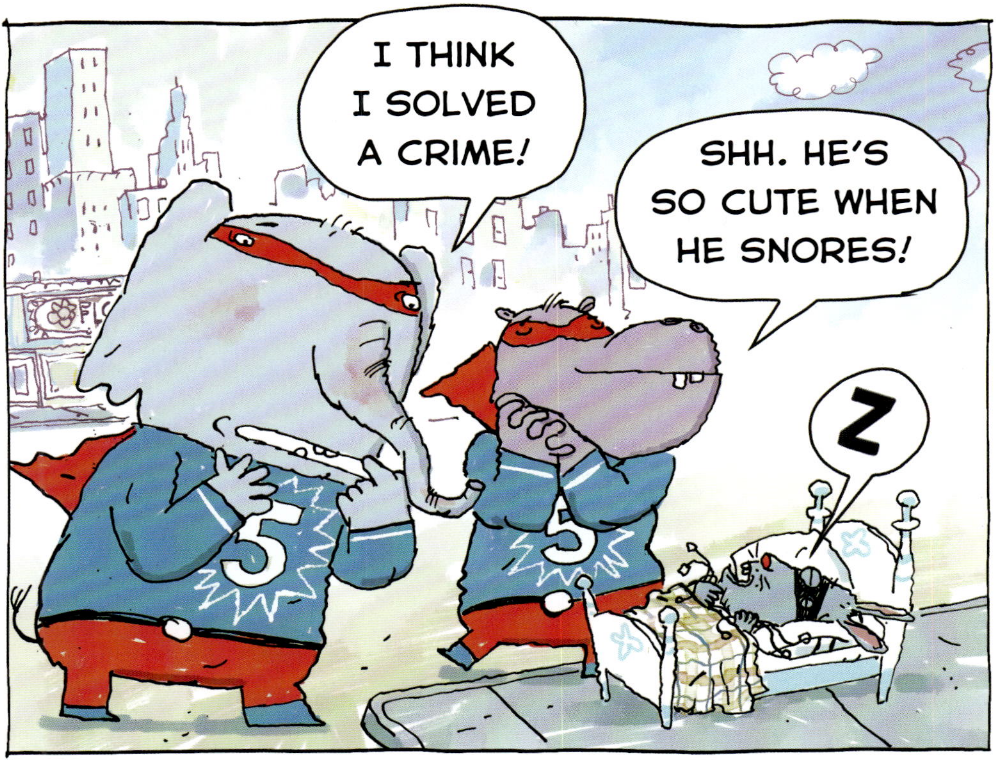
I THINK I SOLVED A CRIME!
SHH. HE'S SO CUTE WHEN HE SNORES!
Z

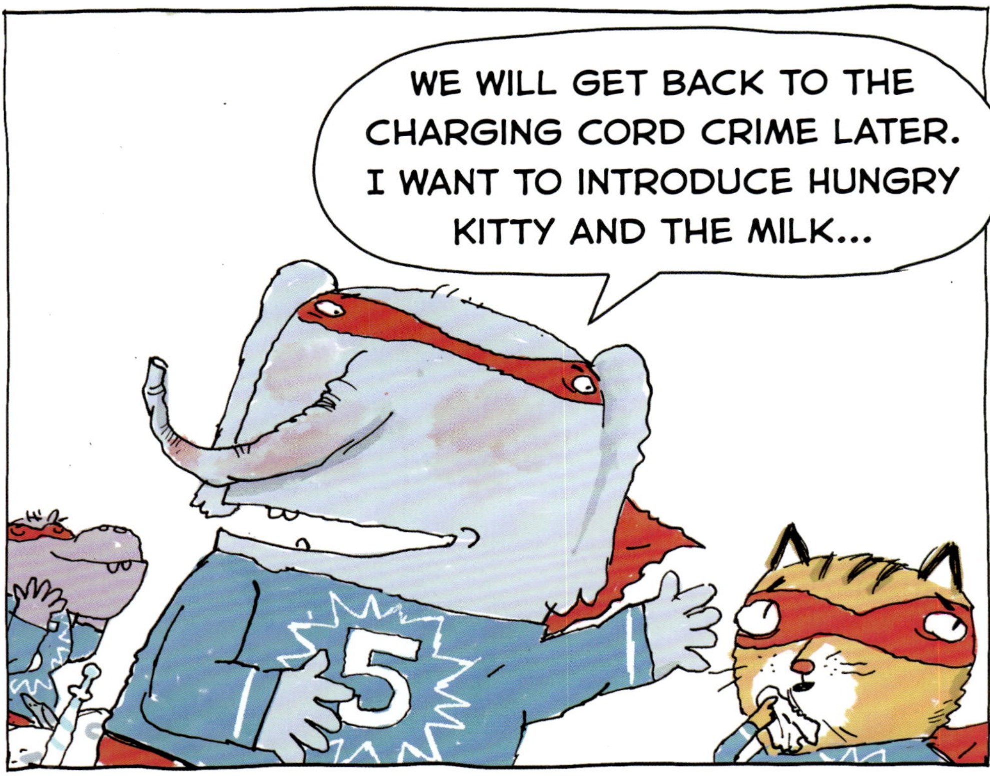
WE WILL GET BACK TO THE CHARGING CORD CRIME LATER. I WANT TO INTRODUCE HUNGRY KITTY AND THE MILK...

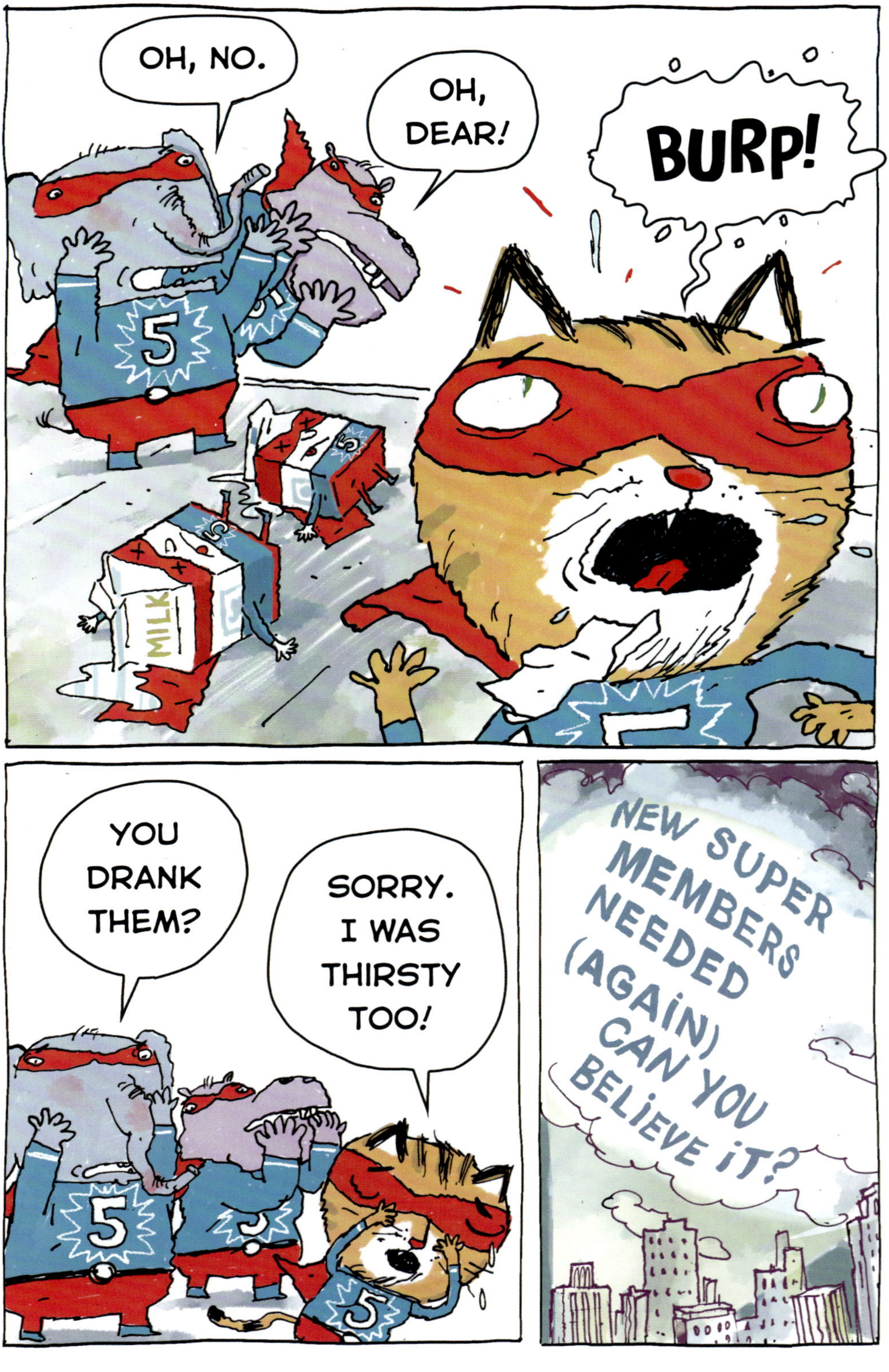
OH, NO.
OH, DEAR!
BURP!
MILK
YOU DRANK THEM?
SORRY. I WAS THIRSTY TOO!
NEW SUPER MEMBERS NEEDED (AGAIN) CAN YOU BELIEVE IT?

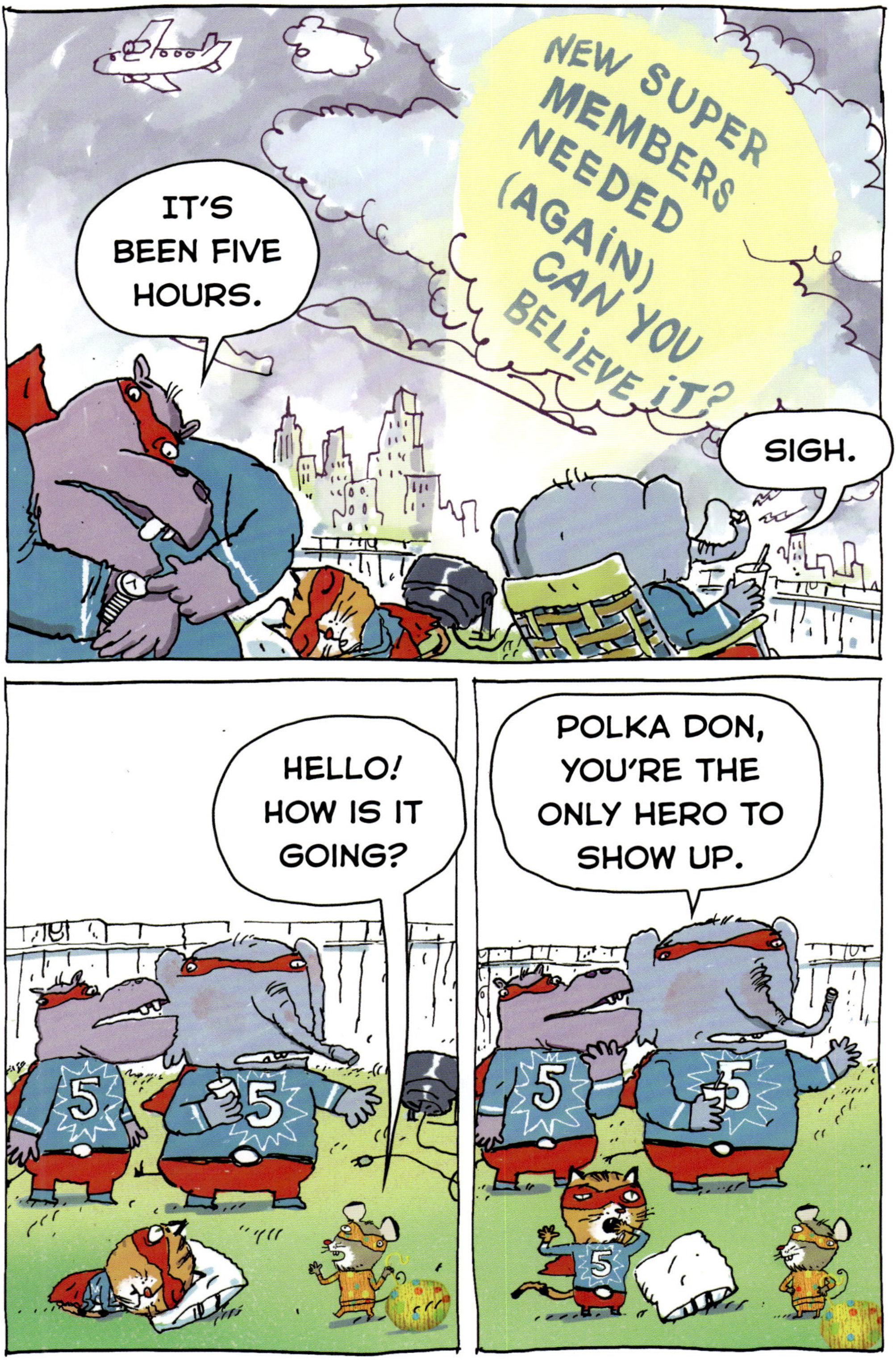
NEW SUPER MEMBERS NEEDED (AGAIN) CAN YOU BELIEVE IT?
IT'S BEEN FIVE HOURS.
SIGH.
HELLO! HOW IS IT GOING?
POLKA DON, YOU'RE THE ONLY HERO TO SHOW UP.

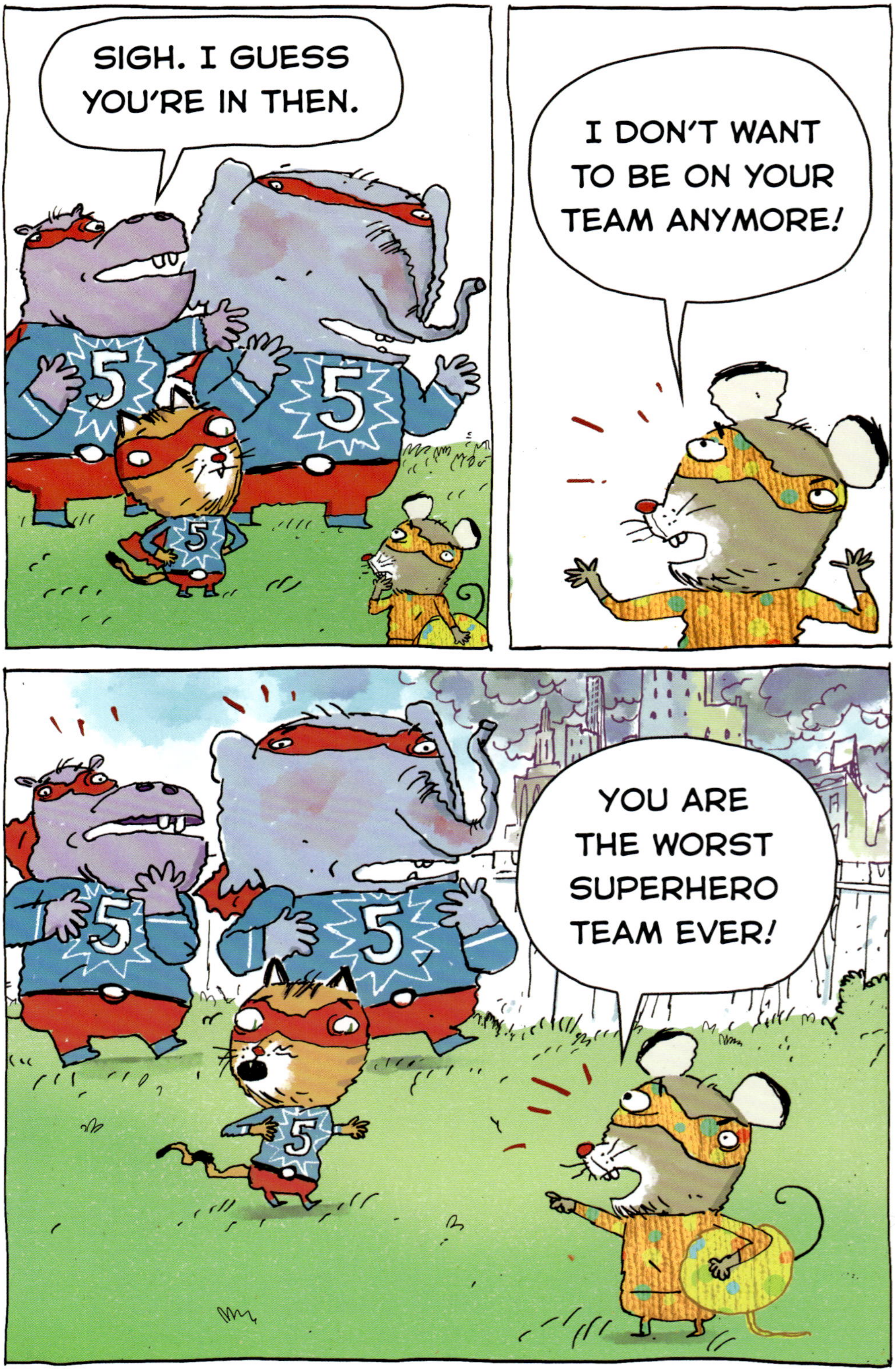
SIGH. I GUESS YOU'RE IN THEN.
I DON'T WANT TO BE ON YOUR TEAM ANYMORE!
YOU ARE THE WORST SUPERHERO TEAM EVER!

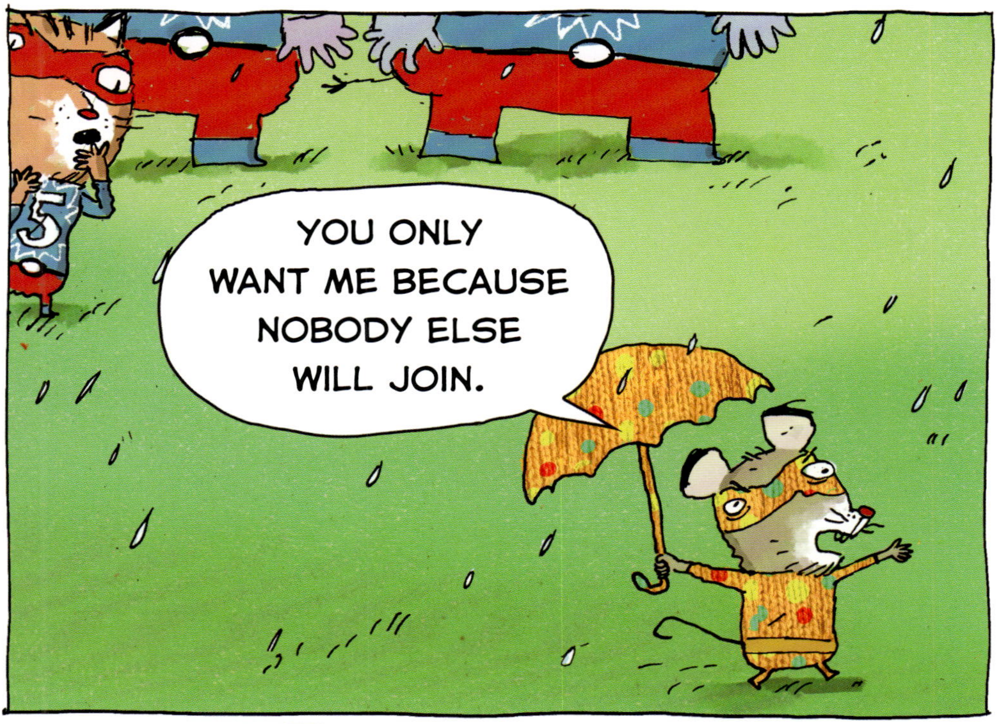
YOU ONLY WANT ME BECAUSE NOBODY ELSE WILL JOIN.

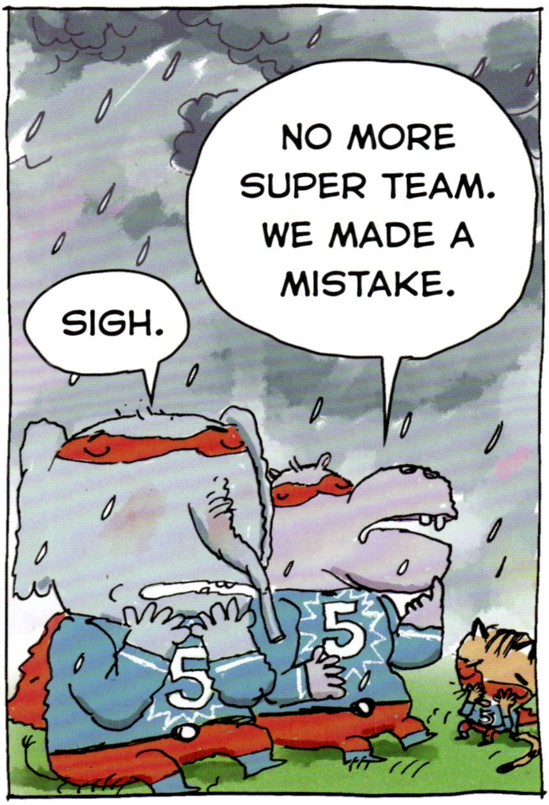
NO MORE SUPER TEAM. WE MADE A MISTAKE.
SIGH.

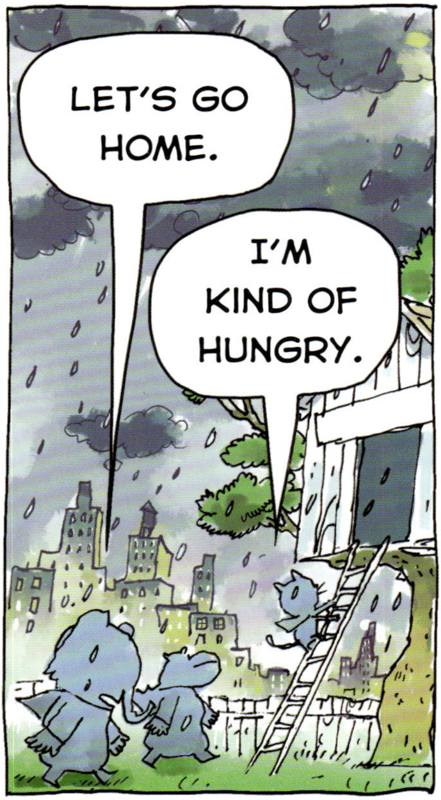
LET'S GO HOME.
I'M KIND OF HUNGRY.

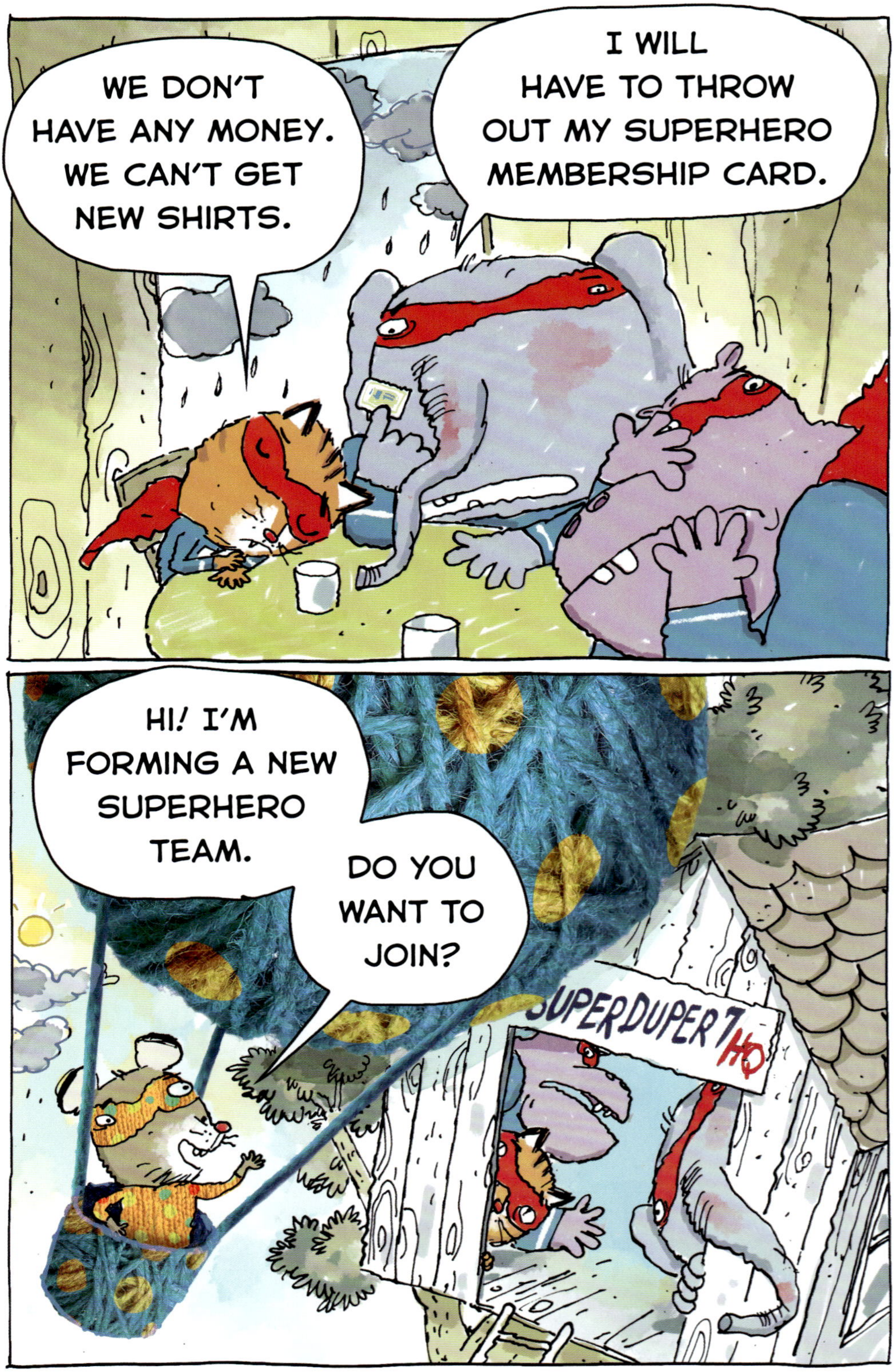
WE DON'T HAVE ANY MONEY. WE CAN'T GET NEW SHIRTS.
I WILL HAVE TO THROW OUT MY SUPERHERO MEMBERSHIP CARD.
HI! I'M FORMING A NEW SUPERHERO TEAM.
DO YOU WANT TO JOIN?
SUPERDUPER 7 HQ

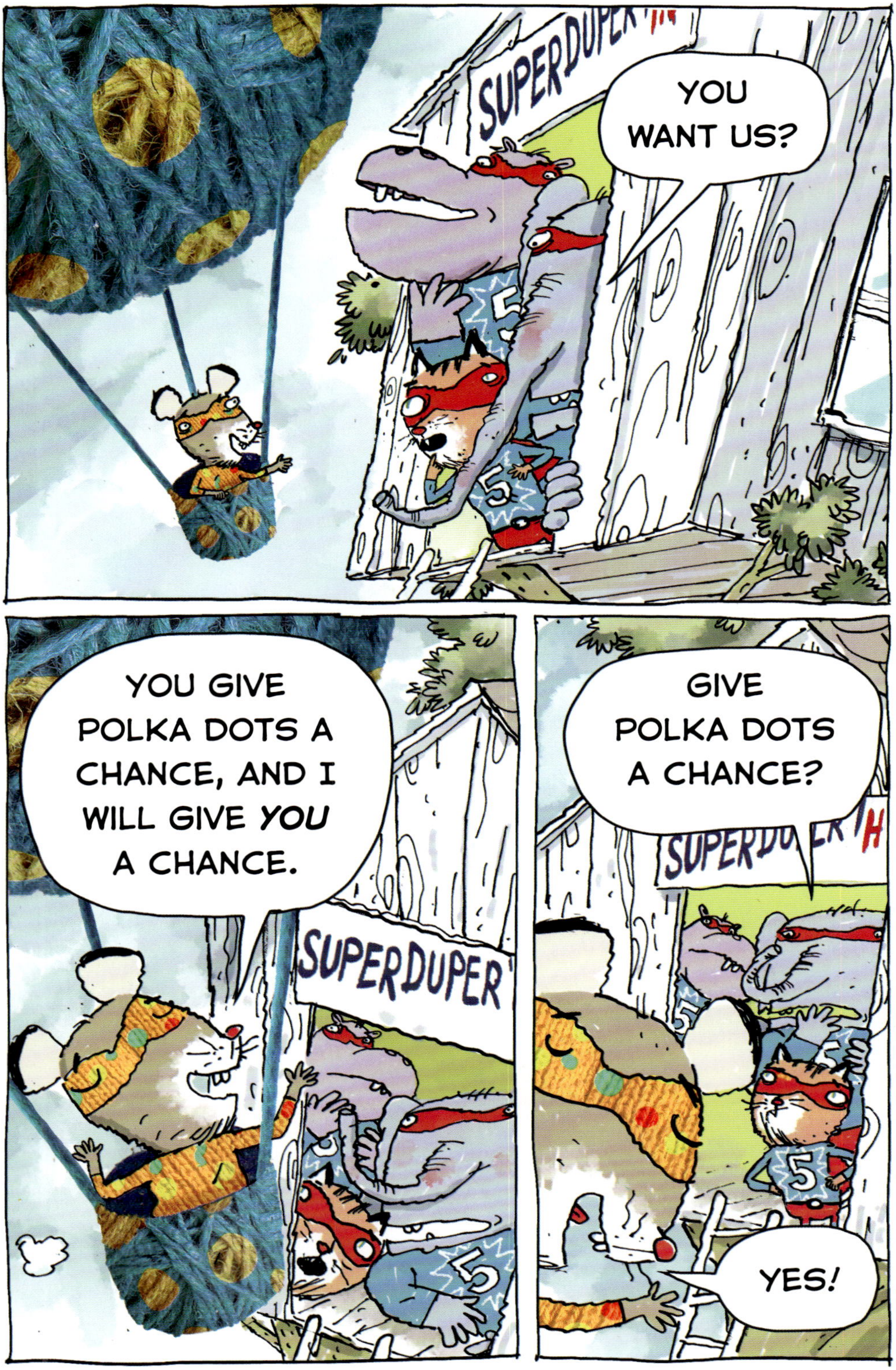
SUPERDUPER
YOU WANT US?
YOU GIVE POLKA DOTS A CHANCE, AND I WILL GIVE *YOU* A CHANCE.
SUPERDUPER
GIVE POLKA DOTS A CHANCE?
YES!

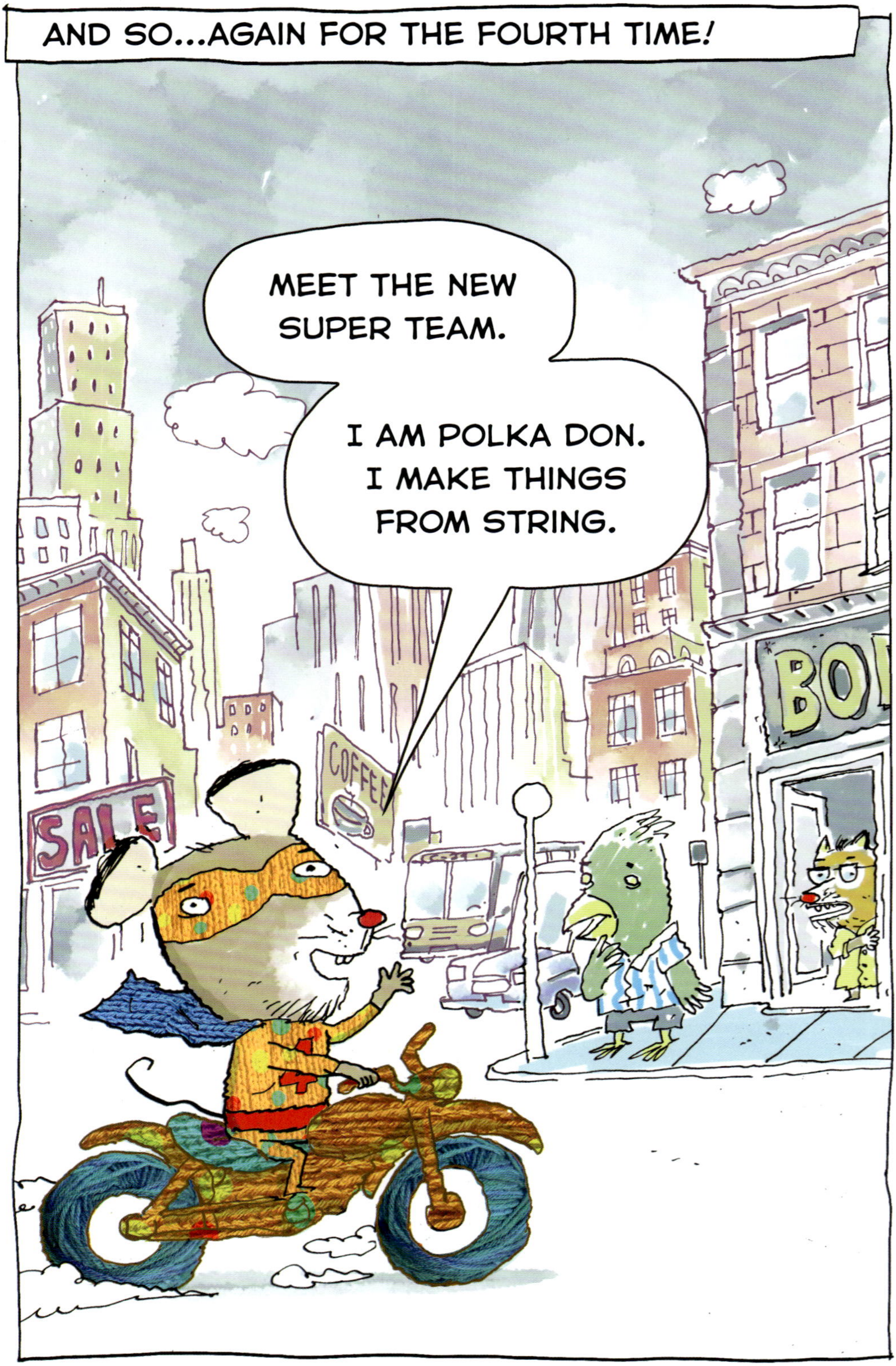
AND SO...AGAIN FOR THE FOURTH TIME!
MEET THE NEW SUPER TEAM.
I AM POLKA DON. I MAKE THINGS FROM STRING.
SALE
COFFEE

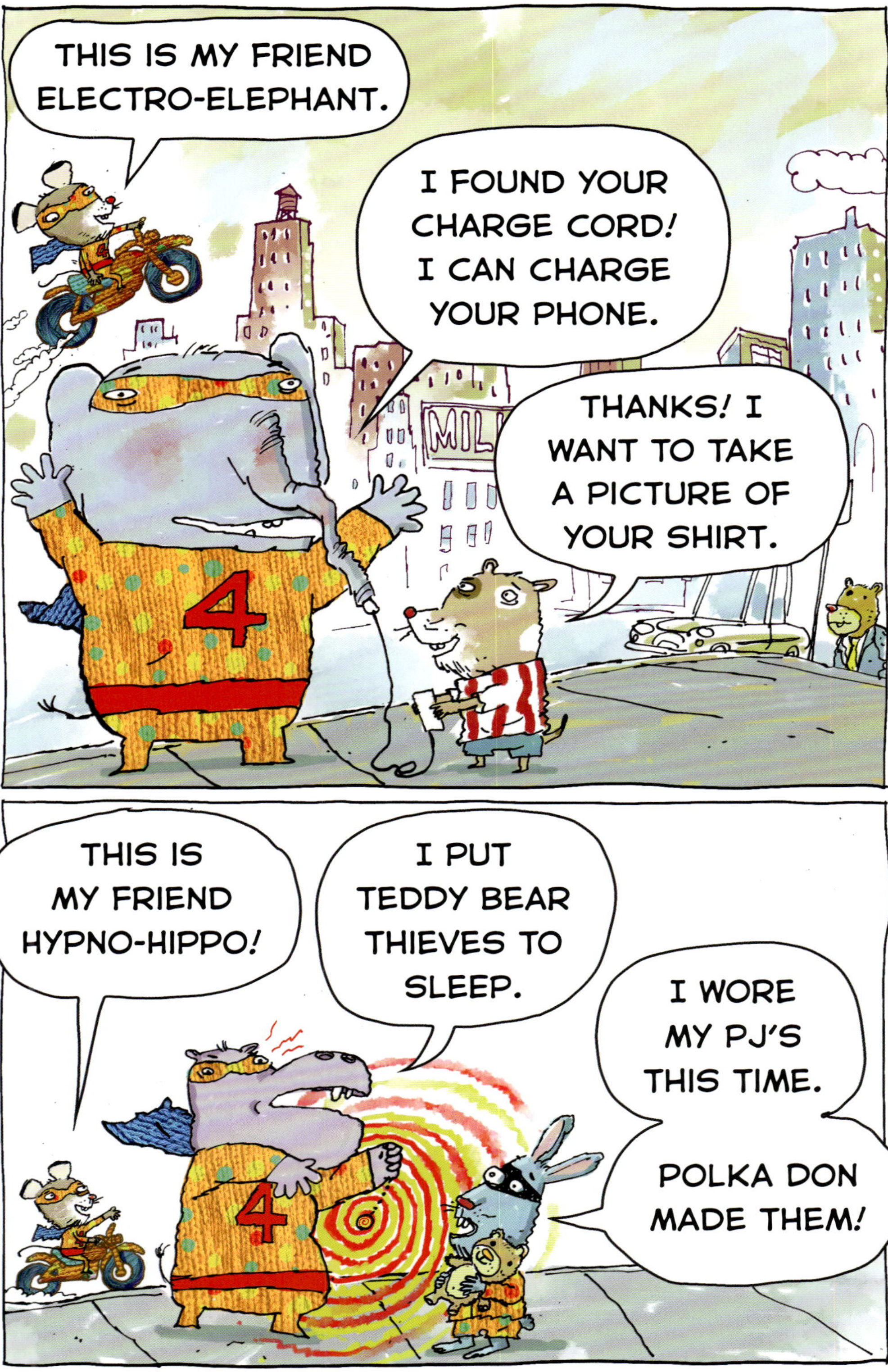
THIS IS MY FRIEND ELECTRO-ELEPHANT.
I FOUND YOUR CHARGE CORD! I CAN CHARGE YOUR PHONE.
THANKS! I WANT TO TAKE A PICTURE OF YOUR SHIRT.
4
THIS IS MY FRIEND HYPNO-HIPPO!
I PUT TEDDY BEAR THIEVES TO SLEEP.
I WORE MY PJ'S THIS TIME.
POLKA DON MADE THEM!
4

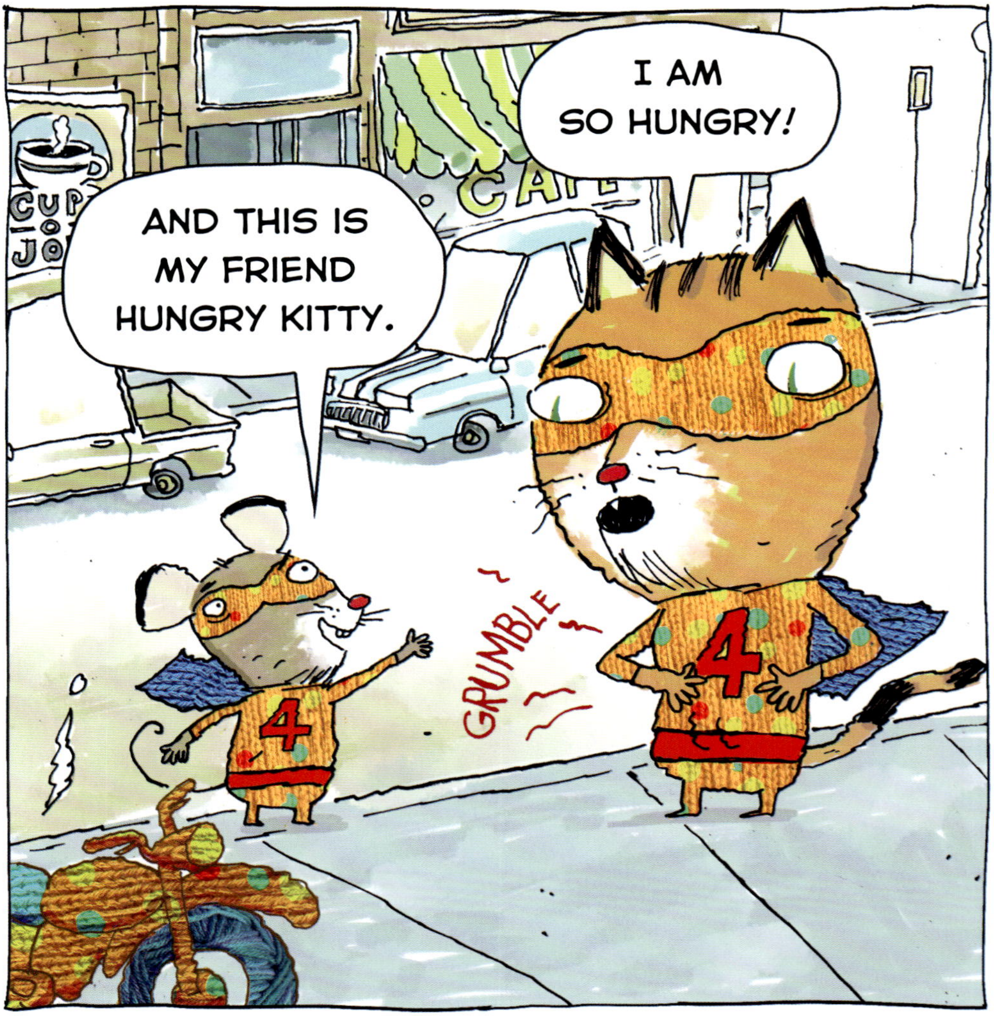
AND THIS IS MY FRIEND HUNGRY KITTY.
I AM SO HUNGRY!
GRUMBLE
CUP O JO
CAFE

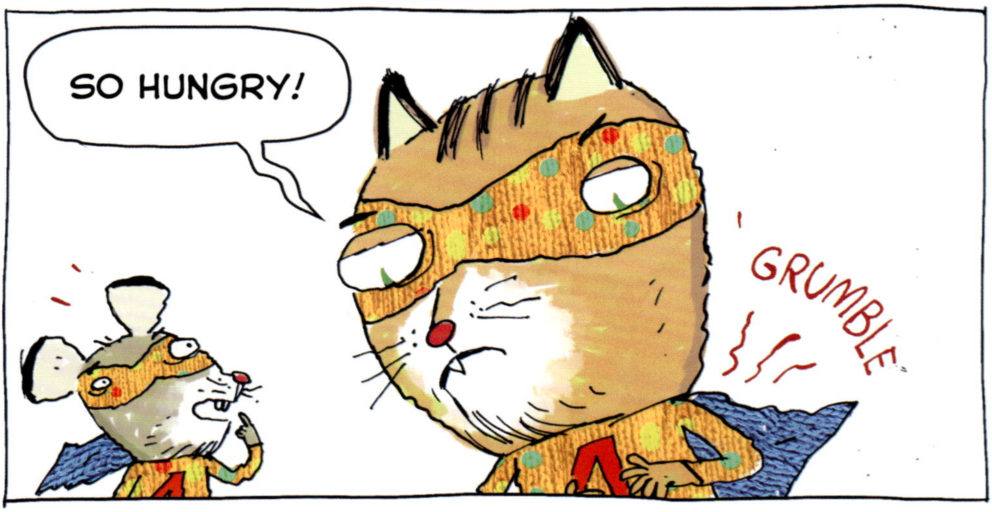
SO HUNGRY!
GRUMBLE

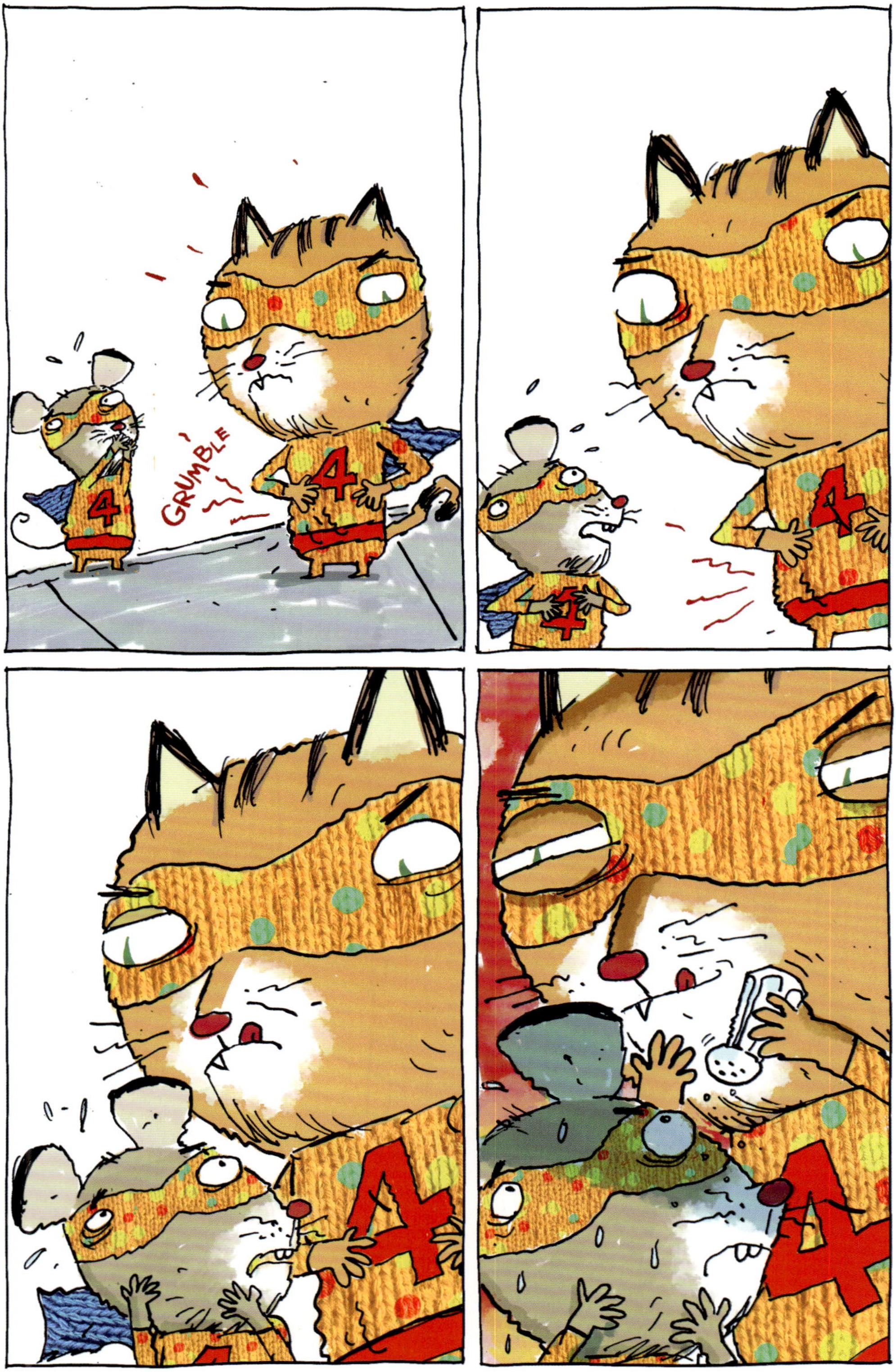
GRUMBLE

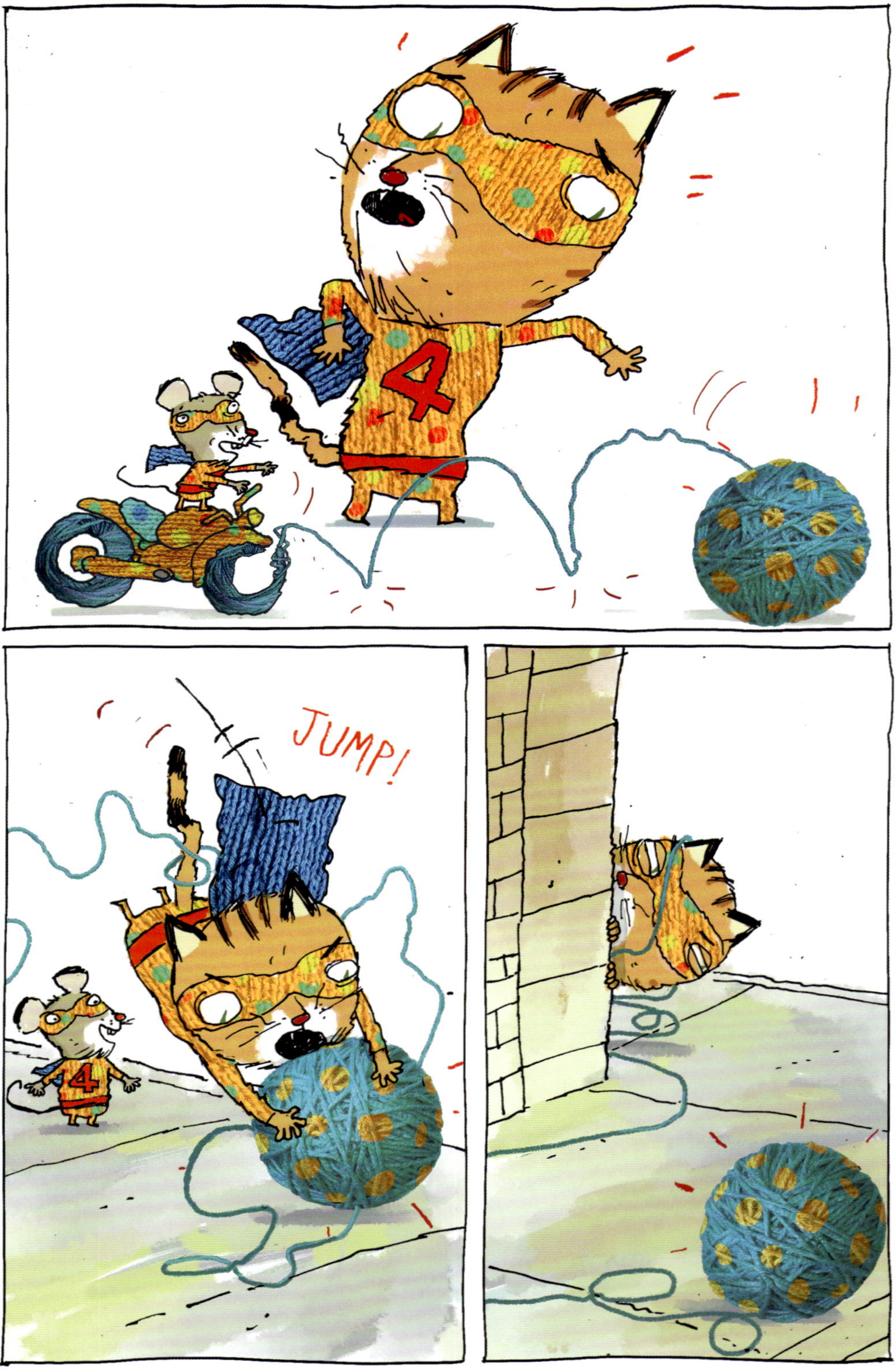
JUMP!

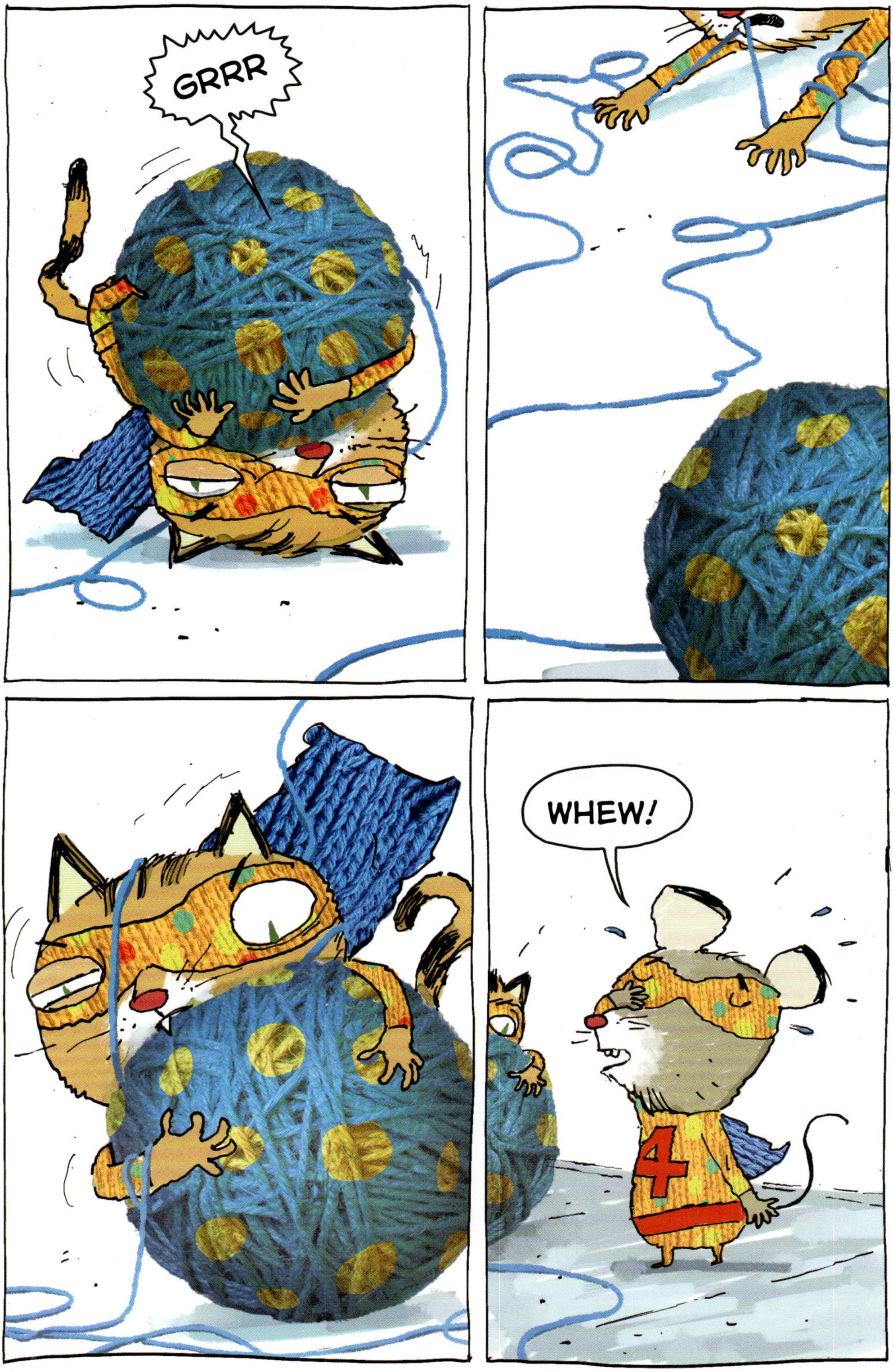
GRRR
WHEW!

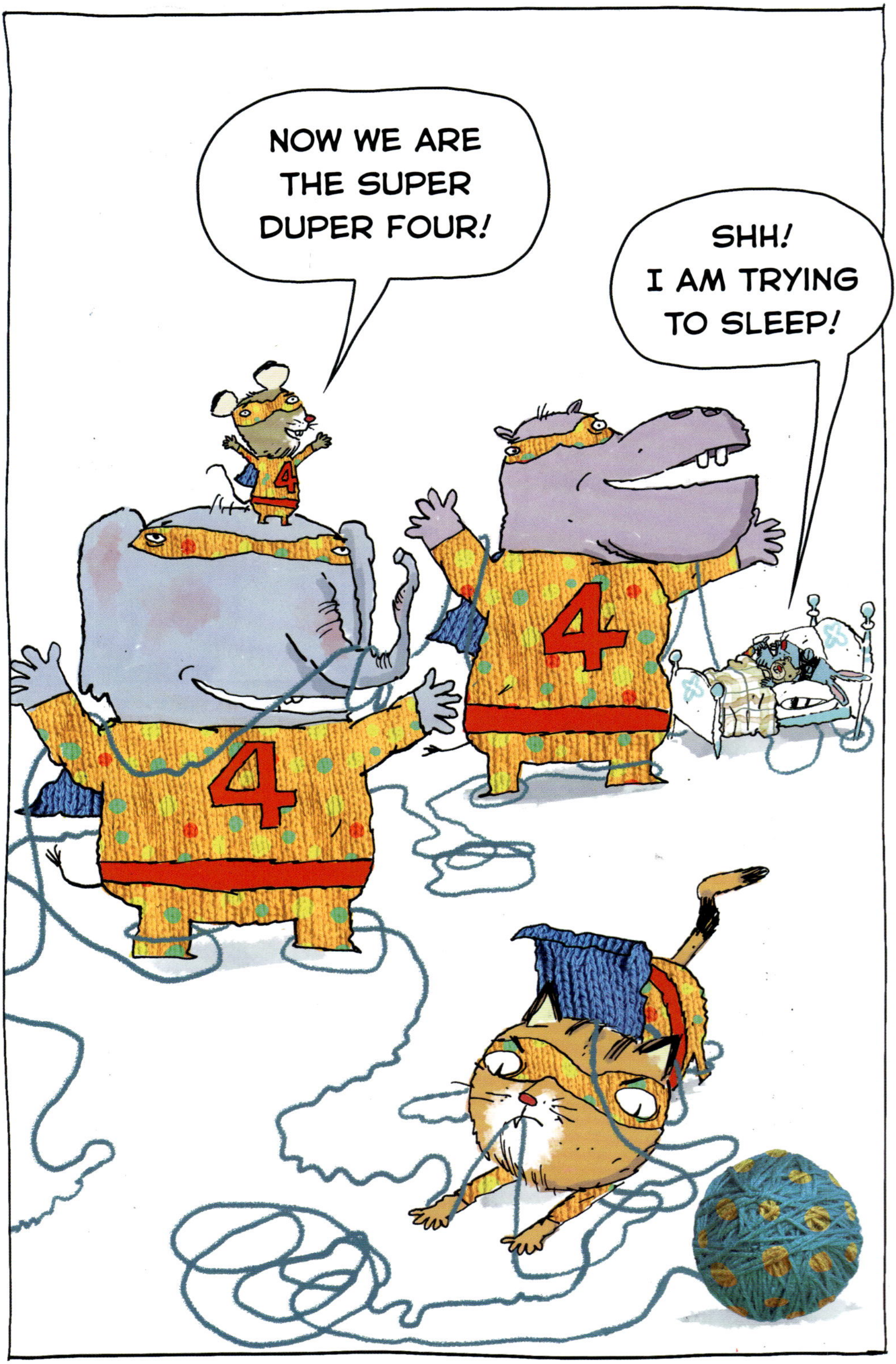
NOW WE ARE THE SUPER DUPER FOUR!
SHH! I AM TRYING TO SLEEP!